OH GOD, THOUGHT BILLY, TOO PARALYZED WITH FEAR TO MOVE. IT'S HAPPENING AGAIN!

Two green, scaly arms burst out of the console, ripping aside control buttons and speaker grilles in a burst of sparks and smoke.

Clawed fingers closed around a technician's throat and pulled him down, bashing his head against the control board. A particularly ugly and nasty gremlin emerged.

A gremlin wearing an evil leer and its multi-colored hair mohawk-style.

"Help me!" the technician screamed in terror.

GREMLiNS 2
THE NEW BATCH

Novelization by DAVID BISCHOFF
Based on the motion picture
written by CHARLIE HAAS
and characters created by
CHRIS COLUMBUS

AVON BOOKS ◆ NEW YORK

AVON BOOKS
A division of
The Hearst Corporation
105 Madison Avenue
New York, New York 10016

First Avon Books Printing: June 1990

AVON TRADEMARK REG. U.S. PAT. OFF. AND IN OTHER COUNTRIES, MARCA
REGISTRADA, HECHO EN U.S.A.

Printed in the U.S.A.

RA 10 9 8 7 6 5 4 3 2 1

This is for
Friz Freleng,
Chuck Jones,
and all the wonderful
writers and animators
of Warner Bros.
cartoons—
And it's in memory
of Mel Blanc.

That ain't all, folks!

Special thanks to Mike Finell, Joe Dante, Betty Moos for wonderful cooperation on the Warner Bros. front. . . . And thanks to Michael Bradley, Elizabeth Martin and Bob Mecoy at Avon Books . . . And thanks to Mike Cassutt, Tom Monteleone and Kim Newman for the Sepulveda Death March that helped make the pressure bearable.

GREMLINS 2

THE NEW BATCH

Chapter
One

It didn't smell like stir-fried cooking or exotic spices tonight in New York City's famous Chinatown.

No, it smelled like money.

Or that's the way it smelled to Frank Forster as he opened the door of the black limo that stretched halfway down the street. The hum of neon from restaurant signs, the slap of taxis splashing through puddles, the smell of fresh fish on ice in an open-air market swept into the limo's plush interior.

Yeah. Money.

Forster's shiny black Oxford shoe avoided a pile of doggie business and orange rind, instinctively finding its way to safe purchase on the sidewalk. He stepped out, drinking deep of the money in the air. Clamp was right, Forster thought as he beckoned for his flunkies to hurry up, chop chop, with the gear. If the prime rule of real estate was "location, location, location" then these blocks sure fit the bill. A hop and a half step from New York's city, state and federal government offices, a stone's throw from Wall Street, and dead on the Manhattan Bridge's gate to Brooklyn, the area was a developer's dream.

His gaze swept the area.

He saw lots of dilapidated old buildings, many with GOING OUT OF BUSINESS signs pasted in their boarded-up windows. All bought up by Mr. Clamp.

All except one.

Forster looked dead ahead. A sign reading simply CURIOSITIES hung at an angle, and soft light hinting of home and pipe smoke and incense seeped through colored bead curtains. It was the domicile of a certain Mr. Wing, the only hold-out to the ever-growing grip of Clamp, Inc.

This was the place, all right.

Impatiently, Forster snapped his fingers twice at the already bustling suited men who popped open the trunk of the limo and pulled out a 25 inch television monitor and a digital VCR.

Frank Forster was a sour-faced man with short corporate hair, a top of the line gray Brooks Brothers business suit, and a bright red power tie. Frank Forster got things done. Frank Forster was the a Fax-generation corporate man. Frank Forster got things done yesterday. This was why he was Daniel Clamp's second in command. What that really meant was that he was Clamp Industries' hatchet man.

The entourage trooped down the steps. The lead man, a former Jets linebacker with shoulders big as the Statue of Liberty's, pushed through the door, ringing an announcement bell. The TV toting duo and Forster followed into the shop.

The place was a real mess, a dilapidated junk store with stuffed monkeys hanging from the ceiling, old vellum blocks crammed on shelves, wicker cages scattered about, and a pleasant but ancient smell, as though it had been there even before the Dutch had bought this island for a handful of costume jewelry. Yeah, maybe this was the hole where they stored those famous twenty-four dollars' worth of beads. It felt ancient. Lingering in the atmosphere were faint musical notes like the afterthought of a beautiful simple melody just ended. It put goose-bumps on Forster's generally cold skin.

He shook off the shivers and attended to business.

The proprietor, Mr. Wing, sat in an easy chair fronting an exotically woven rug, looking like a reject from a Kung Fu movie. He was old and he was Chinese, with Fu Manchu chin whiskers and a robe. Aromatic tobacco fumes wafted from a pipe he was smoking.

As henchmen set up the audio-visual

equipment, the boss addressed the shop owner. "Mister Wing?"

The old man nodded politely, his rheumy old eyes sparkling as though in candlelight.

"Daniel Clamp would like to speak to you."

Snap of fingers.

Snap of controls.

Tape whirred, static flashed momentarily onto the wide screen, giving way to an abrupt hi-definition image of a young looking businessman, exuding phosphor-dot enthusiasm and self confidence.

Mr. Wing watched with barely a note of surprise, as though this kind of thing happened all the time.

"Good morning, Mr. Wing. Let's cut through to the key issues, okay? I'm prepared to increase my offer substantially."

The photogenic image of Daniel Clamp was a face known 'round the world, the very portrait of modern American enterprise. It was a young-looking forty, with lights dancing in the eyes and a genuine home-spun cast to the well groomed features.

A greedy Jimmy Stewart.

"Now, Mister Wing," the tape-recorded stereo voice intoned. "You're attached to your business. I appreciate that. I'm attached to my own business. I develop the biggest buildings in New York and you sell, ah," Clamp's corn-fed blue eyes glanced around, as though they could see the knick-knacks populating the shop. "—little things. Fine. But I'm not just talking about money here."

The camera pulled back, revealing an easel beside Daniel Clamp. Propped upon the easel was an architect's rendering of a grandiose lobby in a huge office building.

"Take a look, Mr. Wing." said the buttoned-down tycoon, taping the picture with a gold ball-point pen. "'The Clamp Chinatown Center—Where Business Gets Oriented.' When I put up a building, it's the biggest— it's the newest—it's the best. People are going to be *killing* each other to get into this building—"

Forster started. There was some kind of twittering sound coming from one of those wicker cages over there. Cripes, it sounded like "Tee vee!" Kind of eerie, but not threatening. A rat? No, more of a mouse sound. Forster just ignored it, shrugging his jacket into properly squared shape and straightening his Saks Fifth Avenue tie.

"Now, we've been able to reach an understanding with everyone on the block—except for you. Let me show you what I'm willing to do for you—" The gold pen ball-pointed. "A newsstand and souvenir concession, right here under the atrium. The foot traffic through here is going to make the Pan Am building look like a ghost town."

That should hook the old geek, thought Forster. But when he looked back over, he saw that Mr. Wing was just sitting there regarding Clamp's image as impassively as he might stare at a boring game of Mah Jongg.

"Please let us know when you've made a

decision, Mister Wing," continued Clamp, flashing his self-assured smile. "You know, I believe that there's always an area of agreement that two people can reach."

The picture of Clamp dissolved to the Clamp Corporation's logo, a stylized C hanging like a vise right next to the Earth. The vise tightened, clamping down upon the Earth.

Mr. Wing nodded. "Yes—" he said sagely, as though all the wisdom of mankind resided behind that noble forehead. "A man can always agree with others. It is more difficult to agree with oneself."

Forster blinked,.

"Does that mean you—"

The old Chinaman coughed. It was a hacking deep, almost tubercular cough. It sounded terribly unhealthy.

The coughing subsided and Mr. Wing answered with the utmost dignity and gentleness. "I'm so sorry. Please tell Mister Clamp that the answer is no."

Damn! A flicker of anger twitched on Forster's face. But he was never one to allow his emotions—such as they were—to get in the way of the rapid execution of business.

There were other places to be, other things to do, other business to be busy with.

He snapped around in an abrupt about-face and hurled a final sentence over his shoulder as he marched out the door.

"Keep the TV."

His time was a hell of a lot more valuable than the effort it would take to lug that thing

around. He snapped his fingers and his assis-
tants/henchmen/bodyguards fell in line behind him.

They left Mr. Wing's Chinese curiosity shop
in single file.

Back in the limo, the chauffeur drove off
and merged into the general bustling traffic of
Mott Street.

"I'm sorry that didn't work out, sir," said
the former linebacker in a voice with so much
bottom it seemed to well up from the plush
floor. "I thought he'd like the TV."

The frown on Forster's face was bending up
into a smug smile. He was thinking back. Forster liked what he was seeing on the Instant
Replay in his head.

"You hear that cough?" Forster pulled out
a bottle of Evian mineral water from the portable refrigerator and poured himself a glass.
"The guy must be eighty, maybe ninety years
old." He savored the cold, clear water. "We
can wait. Mr. Wing's yin, I'm afraid, is not
long for this yang!"

The limo turned onto Mulberry Street and
cruised past the cappuccino bars and spa-
ghetti mills of Little Italy. They passed Um-
berto's Clam House, the place where Joey
Gallo had bought the linguini farm, and Frank
Forster, for all his arrogance, shivered
slightly.

Thank God Mr. Clamp hadn't tried to buy
this block out!

*   *   *

In Mr. Wing's Curiosity Shop, static hissed on the 25 inch Zenith high-definition stereo television set.

From a nearby wicker cage, a furry paw reached out and grabbed the control knob.

Gizmo the Mogwai changed the channels, chirping his song of content.

Oh boy! A new toy!

The technicolor picture exploded on the screen and almost knocked the furry little creature back on his dufus. There was a big, brawny guy clutching what the human-creatures called a "bow and arrow" in his muscled arms. He looked like Paul McCartney on steroids. Atop dark Italian pretty-boy features perched a rag tied around the forehead as a sweatband.

Sylvester Stallone in a Rambo movie.

"To survive war," the Prince of Pecs intoned in his unmistakable Flatbush-nasal voice. "You've got to *become* war!"

Gee! Gosh! What was that guy doing! What was he putting on the end of the arrow! He was screwing a metal arrowhead on the tip. He drew the bow back and fired up into the air.

The picture changed to a Russian helicopter, hanging in the air. The arrow connected with the metal underside of the aerial beast.

And—KA-BLAM!

The chopper blew up, bursting into flame and a thousand pieces, littering the jungle below.

Gizmo's eyes went wide. His arms windmilled with excitement and alarm. So much color, so much action! It reminded him of the Light and Lava Falls of the homeworld of the Mogturmen, the inventors of the Mogwai.

"Neat!" he piped in his distinctive little voice.

Mr. Wing strode up forcefully and clicked off the set. He wheeled around to face Gizmo, shaking a withered finger. "Television again! Ai —uh! An invention for fools. Do you not remember the trouble wreaked by the idiots who watch it!"

Gizmo grinned sheepishly and grinned innocently.

What Mr. Wing was talking about was that terrible debacle a few years back in Kingston Falls, way upstate. That was when that traveling salesman and part-time inventor Rand Peltzer bought Gizmo the Mogwai, and brought him home as a Christmas present for his son, Billy.

Gizmo the Mogwai purred at the very thought of his friend, Billy Peltzer. What a nice young human! And his girlfriend, Kate Berringer! So pretty and cuddly! Nice folks! He just felt so bad about what had happened.

Because the humans had made a terrible mistake. Taking care of a Mogwai bears with it grave responsibility.

There were three rules.

Do not expose them to light.

Do not get them wet.

Do not feed them after midnight.

Light hurt Mogwais. That had been no problem with the Peltzers. However, they had let Gizmo get wet. When Mogwais get wet, they reproduce. This in itself was not bad; you just got more Mogwai, perhaps a little more mischevious than Gizmo. However, up in Kingston Falls, those mischevious little new Mogwai that had popped off Gizmo got into some serious snacking—after midnight.

They had become Gremlins.

And then all heck had broken loose....

Gizmo shivered at the very thought. His little mouth bent sadly into the most forlorn frown.

"Don't you remember! I had to come and take you away! Those small town fools! They almost ruined their own homes! They almost destroyed their own planet! They did not have the...wisdom...(cough) and the fortitude (cough cough) to take the responsibility—"

The ancient Mr. Wing broke into a series of the most awful coughs that Gizmo had heard yet! He bent over double, wracked with spasms and hacking coughs.

The Mogwai's little heart almost broke to see his beloved Mr. Wing hurting so.

If there was only something he could do.

"I am not feeling so well," said Mr. Wing, turning away. "I shall go and have some green tea. And then I shall take a nap. Please, little one, do not get into trouble!"

The unwell little man shuffled off into a dim corner of his shop.

Gizmo the Mogwai sang sadly.

His beloved Mr. Wing was sick!

Gizmo would do anything, *anything* to make him better.

But what could a poor Mogwai do?

The little creature began singing a gayer song. Maybe a nice tune would heal Mr. Wing's spirit, if not his body.

And it was a person's spirit, of course, thought Gizmo, that really mattered.

The beautiful song filled the curiosity shop like sweet perfume.

Chapter
Two

Inside the Clamp Center, world headquarters of the Clamp Corporation, were
hundreds of offices and stores and suites and
the usual array of services for big business.
However, the Clamp Center distinguished itself from other office skyscrapers by including
a good deal more than most others. What other
office centers after all, sported chiropractors
cheek to backbone with fortune tellers; what
other skyscrapers housed the Flat Earth Society right next to a flying saucers society. For
it was Daniel Clamp's policy: if you had the
bucks (and they were big enough) you were
more than welcome to rent space in this, the
Cadillac of modern architecture (Clamp
would have preferred "Rolls Royce" but he
decided that it would be politic to keep

things, at least on the surface, American). Another of the things that the Clamp Center had
that most other office buildings lacked was a
whole floor of television and radio studios,
which produced and broadcast programs for
the Clamp Cable Network.

In one of the tape-editing rooms of the
Clamp Cable Network, a producer named
Mack Shander watched the playback of one
of the day's news stories, a piece on the death
of a certain honorable Asian gentleman, re-
cently deceased.

"Mister Wing's death removes the last obstacle to developer Daniel Clamp's long-
delayed Chinatown project—"

"Okay," said the producer to the editor.
"Switch over to the boss."

The editor made the appropriate adjust-
ments to the bank of shiny knobs, and an image swept across the bank of monitors.

"It is obviously a sad occasion," said the
pre-recorded image of Daniel Clamp. His jaw
stuck out bravely, and the suggestion of tears
of grief glimmered in his eyes. "But the bright
side is that we can go ahead with something
that will mean a great deal to the community
down there..."

Mack Shinder turned down his audio. He'd
heard the spiel before, and besides he was
pretty sick of Clamp's Henry Fonda-meets-
Godzilla voice.

He turned to see Phil Marcus, the reporter
who had done the location shoot in Chinatown, enter the editing room.

"Hey, Mack."

"Hey Phil. Nice piece. I think the juxtaposition is interesting."

"Yeah, but I tried not to make it too obvious. Gotta feed the landlord, you know."

"Cripes, don't I. My West Side duplex rent just got hiked." He sipped at his cup of coffee.

The reporter nodded toward the screen, which had just filled with the image of Chinatown. "That old guy had some neat stuff in his store. You think they'll auction it off or something?"

"You kidding me? The scuttlebutt is that Forster had the bulldozers poised, just waiting for this moment. As soon as the old man croaked, he was ready for serious demolition."

"What, just in case Wing decides he's not really dead?"

"Let's just say that Forster doesn't take chances."

Indeed, that was not far wrong, for even as they spoke, with the camera crews packed and gone, the wrecking ball descended.

Unfortunately, a certain little Mogwai by the name of Gizmo was still in his wicker cage, still inside Mr. Wing's curiosity shop.

Gizmo sighed, and he sang his song again.

It was a very sad song now, in minor key, and it was sad because he missed his friend and keeper Mr. Wing so much. The little creature was in mourning now. He wore a little black arm band around his furry arm and he was bent over, hugging himself, feeling lost and alone.

A tear dripped from one of the Mogwai's wide eyes and dripped down to glisten on the tip of his nose. It fell onto one of the wicker threads of his cage.

Ka - BOOOOM!

The walls of the shop shuddered as though struck by an earthquake. Plaster rained down.

Then a wood support beam fell down and hit the wicker cage, splitting it open. As the whole world seemed to be caving in on him, Gizmo the Mogwai decided that it would be a great idea to get the heck out of there.

He raced away from a falling piece of ceiling, jumped over a smashed hookah, dodged an old record player.

Behind him a large metal wrecking ball crashed through the wall, a mighty behemoth of destruction.

And it was heading his way.

He hopped around and ran for all he was worth.

The wrecking ball seemed to be gaining on him, and to the poor diminutive Mogwai it looked as big as a planet.

Yikes! It was just inches away! Gizmo could feel the cushion of air it pushed in front of it, could imagine the cold of that awful metal ...

At the very last moment possible, the Mogwai leaped away from the flying ball, rolling off to the right and crashing softly into a basket of Indian scarves.

More rending and tearing sounded as the

ball whacked through the next wall. Instinctively, Gizmo realized that he couldn't hide there. This whole building was coming down around his ears ...

He had to get out!

Quickly his little legs sped him out through the gaping hole the wrecking ball had provided. He raced out into the alley, huffing and puffing as falling bricks clicked and clacked behind him, raising a cloud of dust. The Mogwai ran and ran, frightened out of his poor little mind, until he finally reached a part of the alley that seemed relatively calm and quiet.

He took in a deep breath and sighed.

"Hey Joe! Look what we've got here!"

Startled, Gizmo wheeled around and looked up. A pair of rough and callused human hands were reaching down. Gizmo got an impression of a swarthy face with a cigar butt sticking from its mouth.

And then the strong hands grabbed him and held him firm.

Billy Peltzer usually didn't hate anything or anybody. He hadn't even hated the late and unlamented Mrs. Deagle who'd wanted to put his dog Barney to sleep and had ended up as a UFO hurling through the skies above Kingston Falls. No, Billy Peltzer loved animals, he loved sunsets, he loved his mother and his father and his relatives and most of all he loved Kate Berringer, his fiancée.

But Billy Peltzer hated New York City.

Where else, though, did an architect/artist have a chance for success? Where else but Manhattan could Kate hope to succeed, really *succeed* at the career she had chosen—editing books. Of course, she hadn't even really even gotten into the door of that profession yet, but here, in the heart of American publishing, she actually had a chance. True, she was just a tour guide now at the Clamp Building. But hadn't Johnny Carson and Willard Scott started as pages for NBC? Before you knew, Billy was confident that Kate would be first an assistant, then an editor at Clamp Books on the 13th floor of the Clamp Center.

Anyway, though, it was difficult thinking about your dreams when you were in the middle of a New York City rush hour.

Billy Peltzer hated New York City rush hours.

"I should be finished by six tonight," said Kate Berringer as they strode through the outright madness of early morning Times Square. "If we go straight from work, we can make the Early Bird Special at the movies."

They had just emerged from the Times Square subway station, having rattled in on the number 3 IRT train. They elbowed through a crush of office workers, past vendors, hookers, three-card monte artists and the usually effluvia of weird Times Square characters standing outside theatre lobbies of questionable movie houses. It had that trademarked New York day smell about it—that spring thaw smell of roasting chestnuts, concrete, dampness, trash, with just a whiff of various people's cologne or perfume and the stench of the homeless thrown in for good measure.

Billy always walked watching the ground in these kind of areas. You had to watch that you didn't step in something.

"It's going to be close," he said. "Maybe we could do it tomorrow—no, tomorrow's when the Futtermans are coming to town to visit. They really are looking forward to their big city trip!"

Kate dodged a madly careening business man doubtlessly headed for some power breakfast. "Mister Futterman must be getting better if he can travel." Kate wore a bright blue blazer. Upon the lapel was the Clamp ID badge, a Universal Bar-Code stamped on the trademark Big C. It was identical to the one that Billy wore.

"Yeah. His wife says that he's better—it's just that he was so rattled."

"And then the Gremlin Siege of Kingston Falls!" Kate shook her head, disbelief still in those gorgeous deep brown eyes. "I guess having a bunch of monsters driving a snow plow through your living room could kind of do that to you. He almost got killed."

"Right." Billy checked his watch. "We're gonna be late. Maybe we'd better take a cab the rest of the way!"

Of course, even surburban boy Billy realized that the chance of getting an empty cab in New York rush hour was somewhat the same as that proverbial snowballs in that proverbial hot place, but then why not try! God knew if Marla caught him late again, she'd ream him out and hang him up to dry, and while the notion of his very attractive boss paying physical attention was not terribly displeasing, the actual physical pain involved soon would be.

As it happened, a businessman in a trench coat was just getting out of a cab. Billy dashed over and stuck his head into the driver's window to make sure that he got the guy's attention. He was rewarded with a blast of onions and garlic sufficient to knock a bird off a building at fifty feet.

"Thanks. Can you wait a second for my girl-friend." .

The foreign driver squinted and took his stubby cigarette out from under his bushy mustache. "You gooo-eeeeen to dee airport?"

"No, the Clamp Center. It won't take long. It's just up Madison and then—"

The driver almost cut off Billy's nose, he rolled the window up so fast. The cab scooted off back into traffic, leaving Billy choking on a plume of exhaust.

Kate caught up with him and pulled him back out of the traffic before he got creamed by a car, a bus, or one of those crazy bike messengers screaming past breaking the sound barrier.

"Billy...I don't think we're getting the hang of New York City!"

Billy just sighed, dazed at the whole thing.

They walked the eight blocks or so to the Clamp Center and with each step on the filthy concrete, each scabby palm that was stuck in his face demanding spare change, Billy grew more and more depressed.

Cripes, Marla was going to *kill* him!

Pretty soon they approached the incredible monument to power and wealth that was the Clamp Center. Even now, Billy Peltzer always got a little *frisson* when he looked up at the Clamp Center. A monument to late twentieth century architecture, to wealth and power, it rose up like a direct plug into the sky-vault of God Himself. Its freshly scrubbed windows shone, and its metal gleamed. At the base was the ultimate sign of status and power—a huge atrium three stories high. This was the home not merely of trees, but of the Clamp Center Concession Mall. A credit card shopper's paradise, this was Daniel Clamp's fancy offering to the Goddess of Commerce at whose purse-strings he worshiped.

But boy, this building was tall! Boy was it beautifully built. Clamp had gotten the absolute best architects to design it, used only the best materials. It had a status address in a status city. Rumors were that a cleaning lady had once spotted Daniel Clamp in his office at the tippy top of the Tower, leaning out the window, screaming, "Top of the World, Ma!"

Almost at the doors, Billy turned to Kate.

"You know that painting I'm doin' now— the big building in Chinatown? It's really driving me nuts."

"Why—what's wrong?"

"Like yesterday—I had it looking really good, and then my boss told me to take 20 stories off the World Trade Center so our building looks taller."

"Wow, that's pretty dishonest!"

"Yeah, no kidding...I don't think I'm getting that promotion this year."

"That's okay. We don't have to wait."

"Yeah we do. It wouldn't feel right, getting married on the money I'm making now. It's bad enough that you got me the job!"

Kate turned on him, hand on hip. Her hair was shorter now, and she looked older, but in a very appealing, very clean and honest way. Billy just always hoped that the city never made her hard and cold. The sweet, naive Kate was so much more appealing. "I didn't *get* you the job, I just *heard* about it. Billy, you can get promoted and stuff if you want to, but you have to act like you deserve it. Let people know you're *there!*"

Yeah, thought Billy as they approached the revolving doors. Maybe she was right. He was kind of the wallflower in his office. He should probably be more assertive...It was just that he didn't like playing office politics and brown-nosing, like Marla did.

"Want to try the revolving doors today?"

Kate looked at the supersonic high-tech doors with extreme suspicion. "I don't know. I had a big breakfast this morning..."

Even as they stood contemplating the venture, a red-faced executive with a briefcase rudely elbowed past them and dived into the revolving doors.

He was promptly spun round as fast as the Tasmanian Devil on a hungry day and tossed head over heels back onto the apron in front of them, legs and arms akimbo and tangled up in the spilled papers of his briefcase.

"Uhm—you're right," said Billy.

So they used a regular door, a door marked PLEASE USE REVOLVING DOORS, instead.

They entered the lobby, and the change was profound. From the New York rush hour hell they entered a temperature-controlled Heaven, a paradise of modern scent and high-tech texture. This ultra-modern, monumental-style lobby included bars, restaurants, a frozen yogurt stand, a beauty parlor, clothing stores and enough shoe stores to satisfy even Billy Peltzer's mom. Only of course, all this was all upscale. Chi-chi. Posh. A number of the people who walked through this carpeted environment could be recognized instantly as Clamp employees by their bar code ID tags shaped like Big Cs—the same as Billy and Kate wore.

Kate waved hello to an attractive thirtyish woman leading a tour group, rubber-necking the lobby and clicking pictures of this monument to magnificence. Billy recognized her. She was a friend of Kate's named Doreen who had the same job as Kate. She wore the same sharp blue uniform as Kate, with a tall hat modeled on the Clamp Building sticking up.

"... hope you've enjoyed your tour of the

world's most modern automated office building. Don't forget, copies of Mr. Clamp's best-selling book, I TOOK MANHATTAN, are on sale at the newstand.''

Kate turned back to Billy. "Don't let things get to you."

"I won't."

They kissed and while Kate's lips were soft and full on his for a moment, he forgot his troubles.

It was these times that made all this New York craziness worthwhile.

Billy scooted off to catch the next elevator up.

Unfortunately, he just missed it.

A soothing electronic voice greeted his button-push.

"Thank you for pushing the elevator button."

Oh great, thought Billy. More time for Marla to stew.

Then a man came into the lobby who made Billy Peltzer tense up tight as . . .

Well, tight as a clamp.

Chapter
Three

Frank Forster, Daniel Clamp's hatchet man supreme, walked into the lobby of the Clamp Center looking as though he owned the place. He was just that kind of a guy, with his straight arrow poise, his dark Clint Eastwood looks, and his eyes cold as flint at the bottom of a mineshaft.

As he walked hurriedly through the lobby, his belt page suddenly beeped.

Technology was calling.

And when technology called, Frank Forster answered, pronto.

He changed direction, zooming into an alcove off the lobby where he unlocked a cabinet. This opened to reveal a large hi-res TV screen. Perched above this was a video camera, beaming his stern visage upstairs.

And on the screen of course was Daniel Clamp's face, looking rather impatient.

Yes, when technology called, Frank Forster answered...especially when Daniel Clamp was on the other end of the line!

"Forster," snapped Clamp. "I've got the planning commission people coming in here today. Those condos I want to build, on top of the Chrysler building? We're *this* close to an okay."

"Yes, sir."

"So I want this place running like a clock—the systems, the people, everything."

"Yes sir. I'm doing a decor compliance check this morning. Tonight, I'm doing a random drug search and—"

Forster was interrupted.

"Excuse me, Mister Clamp," came an insistent voice from behind him. "Could I speak with you, Mister Clamp, sir, for just a mom—"

Forster wheeled around.

There, looking like a lost joke out of Halloween party was a man in full-blown Dracula get up. He didn't look like Bela Lugosi, but more like Al Lewis as Grandpa Munster, and just about a third as scary.

This was Grandpa Fred, Forster realized immediately, apparently escaped from his coffin in Studio E.

"We're busy," snarled Forster in his least pleasant voice.

Grandpa Fred attempted to get around him. "I just need a—"

Forster slammed the cabinet shut.

"I *said*—we're *busy*."

"Well, gosh, Mr. Forster. All I wanted to do was to actually speak to Mr. Clamp." An attempt at a winning smile on Grandpa Fred's face fizzled. "Doesn't anybody but you get to talk to him—"

"Unless you care to get shipped back to the Borsht Belt, Grandpa, you'll get your cape and your fangs outta my face."

Grandpa Fred, crushed, shlepped away, cape dragging behind.

Forster shook his head and opened up the cabinet again to continue his electronic tête-à-tête with his beloved boss.

As Billy waited impatiently for the elevator he recognized a familiar perfume and his spine turned rigid.

Marla Bloodstone, the head of his department, a.k.a. his boss, was also waiting.

"Billy . . ." she said.

"Hi, Marla, How—"

Marla was smoking, as usual. She interrupted as usual, her words coming out punctuated by puffs of cigarette smoke. "Your Chinatown drawing. We have to have it. It's a crisis panic emergency. The printers are killing us—"

Marla was clearly in her usual state of hyper, coffee-fed melodramatic tension. She was New York frantic in the most emphatic manner possible. She was a pretty, nice figured woman who might have had more sex appeal but for her severe business suit, her flossed

red hair and the tons of make up that made
it look like her face was lacquered on.

Otherwise she looked like that cute lady in
the American Express commercial who takes
her big brother out to dinner.

"Oh yeah. The drawing. I just have to—"

She tugged him onto the elevator, cram-
ming in with a bunch of other office workers.

"Please state your desired floor number,"
requested the soft computer voice politely.

Marla said, "I've got *thirty two* people
screaming at me for—"

The "thirty two" was so emphatic that it
overrode her neighbor worker's feeble attempt
at "sixteen."

"Your request is floor thirty two."

"No, no, not thirty two!" screeched the
worker, probably late himself.

"No," said Billy, alarmed. This had happened before. "Don't!"

But it was too late.

"You have cancelled floor thirty-two," intoned the elevator-voice portentiously.

It stopped in mid-rise, quite abruptly and
violently, heaving its occupants around, mixing them up like tossed-people-salad.

"Please state your new desired floor number."

"Fifty eight!" said Marla, before anyone
else got a chance to pitch their numbers.

"Your new request is fifty-eight."

The elevator started again, even as the other
passengers hurled their orders.

Marla shrugged. Realizing that she had

dropped her cigarette somewhere along the line, she pulled out a pack from her purse with long red nails, tapped a new one out and lit it. Smoke hurled up into the air.

People glared at her.

"Smoking is anti-social," said the computer voice.

"I hate this thing," said Marla.

So did Billy, but then he wasn't crazy about cigarette smoke either.

Although Marla was certainly hyper, she didn't seem to be actually *mad* at him. Bill untensed a bit and, doing so, realized that maybe Marla wasn't all that bad after all. She just had some problems like everyone. Living in this hellhole city all your life was bound to screw you up some. As Billy stood close to his boss in the crowded elevator and considered her in this new light, he realized that she was . . . well, very feminine beneath that office shell. She *did* smell good, and she was really rather attractive.

Billy chastised himself immediately. What was wrong with him! He was engaged to the most wonderful girl in the world, and here he was semi-lusting after his *boss* for goodness sake!

The door opened on their floor.

Billy and Marla shuffled out onto the advertising department of Daniel Clamp Enterprises.

"Listen, this deadline," said Marla in her nasal Brooklyn accent, "It's not my fault. They're making me miserable so I have to make you miserable. It's a complete heart attack disaster horror story!"

This whole floor was the advertising section, and it consisted of ultra-modern "open-plan" offices—endless beige partitions forming tiny cubicles full of "ergonomic" furniture. The company piped in "white noise," low-volume static, through hidden speakers to insulate conversations in the spacious room.

As Billy and Marla walked through they passed a worker who was trying to get a drink from one of the department's designer water fountains. When he pushed the button, the fountain's spigot overshot by several inches, splashing onto the carpet. The worker contorted himself to get a drink, but got his face splashed as the fountain surged.

Billy noted this. The same thing had happened to him just yesterday.

They arrived at Billy's cubicle. His "workstation" consisted of a drawing board, several drawers and a phone equipped with a video screen. A small potted plant struggled to survive. Pinned to the cubicle wall was Billy's drawing of the main street of his hometown, Kingston Falls.

On Billy's drawing board was an illustration of Clamp's projected Chinatown building—a glass monstrosity with insane pagoda touches. Billy had tried to breathe some artistic life into it, drawing people in the street, kids flying dragon kites and people eating from ceramic bowls with chopsticks.

Billy noticed Marla staring at it, arms folded under her ample breasts.

"It's almost finished. I just have to make some—"

"The courtyard looks cold." She poked with the cigarette. "That'll be nicer with trees."

"Are they going to plant trees there?"

"Hell no, but you're going to draw them!"

"But Marla!"

"Elms." She gave him an authoritative glare, and he did not care to challenge her anymore.

"Right."

Billy was about to sit down and get to work but just at that moment Daniel Clamp's lieutenant, Frank Forster, marched down the row of cubicles, his beady eyes surveying.

Suddenly Marla, ever political, was all smiles and good mornings. "Hi, Mister Forster."

Forster nodded at Marla, her attractiveness clearly lost on his metal-plated heart. He ran an eye over Billy's cubicle, grunted and then fixed the young man with a cold stare.

"It looks like somebody hasn't read his employee manual. . . . doesn't it, Mister—"

As he spoke, Forster opened a leatherette folder and took out a bar-code reading wand attached to it by a curled cable. He rubbed the laser-wand over the bar-code on Billy's chest and read from an LCD display in the folder.

"Peltzer," Forster read.

"Uh, what's the problem . . ."

"Unauthorized potted plant." Frank Forster's eyes narrowed. "Possible aphid infestation."

Hastily, Billy crammed the plant into a desk drawer.

Forster spotted Billy's drawing on the partition. "What *is* this?"

"My home town."

"Mr. Peltzer, do you know how much the Clamp organization has spent to provide its employees with art by recognized artists at this facility?"

He pointed to a piece of anonymous "bank art" on a nearby wall—a generic painting of flowers in a vase.

"Eye-resting. Color-coordinated. *Authorized!*"

"Yes sir. It was just a—"

"A little touch, yes. Maybe *everybody* here would like to do some little touches." The severe man leaned closer, so close that Billy could smell his toothpaste. "Coffee mugs that say 'World's Greatest Lover.' The cute little hula doll they bought in Hawaii. The Snoopy comic that just says it *all!* You'd like that, wouldn't you, Mister Peltzer?"

Billy pulled back and looked around. "I don't see any—"

"Coming to work every day in a *two hundred million dollar flea market.*"

Forster sniffed and then moved on, his eagle eyes inspecting the advertising offices.

Marla stewed and fumed—quite literally *fumed*—smoke wafting voluminously from her nicotine stick. She tapped her feet nervously and her eyes darted about as though she was sure, just absolutely no question positive that Daniel Clamp was watching them right this very second!

"Billy this is *just* what I don't need right now. Do you realize we've got department reviews in three weeks? This is a nuclear meltdown disaster. I *mean* it!"

Billy sighed and tried to smile encouragingly. "Sorry, Marla. But you know, it could have been worse."

"Worse. What do you mean worse!" Her bosom heaved emotionally, her arms whipped out melodramatically, spraying ashes all over Billy's work station. "Mister Forster's probably going to put this whole department on report! Just because you've got a messy desk with a vegetable growing on it!"

She stormed away still ranting. "Just straighten it it out, Billy. Just get your act together, huh, for gawd's sake please!"

Billy sighed and hid his drawing of Kingston Falls in his pocket. He wondered how a woman like that would have made out in Kingston Falls a few years ago.

He shrugged and got down to working.

Chapter
Four

Kate Berringer ushered her latest group of tourists through the bustling lobby.

"The Clamp Center is the most advanced 'smart' building in America, with the latest in security, communications and climate control," she said in smart, clipped tones, standing tall and cool and confident as she had been instructed to do always.

She beckoned the group—a typical bevy of gawking tourists in polyester clothing and cheap haircuts—to follow her to a staircase.

"The Clamp Center," she continued, "is just one part of Mister Clamp's round-the-world business network which includes construction, sports, finance, and a popular line of jams and jellies . . . and, of course as those

of you who have cable TV at home know—
Clamp Cable Network!''

Meanwhile, up in the Clamp Cable TV studios, a video image played in one of the control rooms.

The MICROWAVE WITH MARGE SHOW.

Marge, a heavy set woman with a matronly
smile, was even now taking a dish from one
of the numerous ovens on her set.

"... some people have written in to say that,
if they're serving these dishes in a dark room,
maybe for those romantic occasions, they notice a *glow* coming from some of the meat
courses. Now, that's perfectly normal..."

Billy Peltzer watched the image for a moment and then strode past the control room,
carrying a shopping bag. He went down a narrow hallway and stepped next to a particularly run-down set.

This was the set of GRANDPA FRED'S
HOUSE OF HORRORS, the Clamp "Ghost
Host" movie. It consisted of the prerequisite
tilted tombstones—paper mâché, of course—
beside a coffin.

Billy stood beside the cameraman.

Poor Grandpa Fred, he thought. He really
deserves a better shot than this. He'd never
been quite the same since Clamp had bumped
his show out of its primo midnight Saturday
slot to the 3:30 AM slot.

Still, the old trooper was giving his taped
segment his very best shot.

Grandpa Fred walked along, his hands

lifted in predatory fashion, creepy-creeping along the floor from which a weak dry ice fog exuded. His face was turned toward the camera and he hammed it up in royal fashion.

Grandpa Fred did not use a Bela Lugosi accent. Fred's theory was that Grandpa Fred was Dracula's cousin from Dubuque, Iowa. Besides, the only accent he could do was Mexican and that would sound too wierd.

". . . tonight's movie is *so scary*—the people who saw it when it came out in the theaters twelve years ago are just learning how to speak simple phrases and eat solid food again! That's right! Talk about scary! It's a good thing your Grandpa Fred is here with you—"

He lifted his head expectantly, having just cued for a special sound effects.

Nothing happened.

Billy watched as Grandpa Fred straightened, breaking character, and glared up at the control booth with resigned disgust. "So where's the moan?"

The director in the booth answered over the P.A., "The what?"

Grandpa Fred slapped his forehead. "The moan. There's supposed to be a moan from the back and I say, 'Oh, Renfield, you want some more *flies* don't you,' and I go back there and open the door."

"Oh, sorry, Fred," said the director. "Can somebody find the tape with the moan?"

Grandpa Fred sat down, a study in disgust.

Billy hastened over to him to try to cheer him up.

"Hi, Fred! Hey, I was sorry to hear about your new time slot. I think they're making a big mistake."

"A mistake?" Grandpa Fred grunted, all semblance of enthusiasm gone from his manner. "Kid, it's a disaster. People that watch TV at three-thirty in the morning are not scared of the Wolfman. The only thing that scares those people is getting sober and finding work."

"Yeah," Billy agreed. Remembering why he'd come, Billy brightened.

Reaching into his shopping bag, he pulled out the mechanized bat that he'd bought in a knick-knack shop on Columbus Avenue. Fred Stignakowski was just about the only guy in this whole building who'd made friends with him when he started to work for Clamp Enterprises last year. He'd heard about the rotten scheduling change, and he'd wanted to cheer the old guy up.

When Billy started the bat's wings flapping, Grandpa's eyes popped wide open and he held his hands up to protect himself.

"Watch it with that thing!"

Billy stood and placed the bat on top of the cobweb covered TV set behind the coffin.

"I thought it would look good over here."

"Frankly, kid, this was not what I had in mind," said Grandpa Fred, shaking his head, the weight of the world plainly resting on his shoulders. "I wanted to do news. Public affairs. Something *meaningful*."

Billy was upset to see Grandpa Fred looking

so sad. Fred was one of the nicest people that
Billy knew, a salt of the earth kind of guy who
might be running a general store in say...
Kingston Falls. Yeah, Fred would be so much
happier in a smaller town Billy thought. The
big city had just crushed the poor guy's
dreams and broken his heart. Here was a guy
who'd come to the Big Apple hoping for a
piece of the action and gotten a mouthful of
seeds and worms.

Billy groped around for something com-
forting to say.

"Horror movies can be meaningful, Fred.
You should run some of the classics—FRAN-
KENSTEIN, DRACULA..."

Fred's caped shoulders slumped forlornly.
"All the great horror movies are in black and
white. Mister Clamp only likes color. I don't
even have a gimmick. No special effects. A
puppet that comes out of a box—whoopee!
Big deal!"

The director's voice suddenly boomed from
the control room public announcement
speaker. "We've got the moan, Fred."

"OhhhhhhoOOOOOOOOOOOOOhhhhhm-
mmmmmmmmmmmmmmmOOOOOOOOOO-
OH!" issued from the speaker. It was about
as spooky as a whoopee cushion.

An expression of infinite distress crossed
Fred's features.

"That's the moan?"

"That's what we've got, Fred," snapped the
director's voice, its owner clearly losing patience. "And...rolling!"

Grandpa Fred hastily wallowed his way up to standing position. He assumed his character again with the utter professionalism that Billy admired tremendously.

Billy scooted off the set.

"Oh, Renfield," said Grandpa Fred. "You want some nice delicious scrumptious crunchy *flies*? Well, we'll—"

"Whoops," called the director suddenly. "I didn't see what time it was! Sorry, Fred. We'll pick it up right there."

Fred lifted his arms in quiet exasperation, shaking his head and smiling. This was what Billy liked most about Fred. Even in his darkest moment, even when he was clearly depressed as a cat on the wrong side of a steamroller, Fred could see the ironic humor in it all.

They walked out toward the "mall" to get a Clamp Burger.

"Have you seen him?"

"Who Billy?"

"Daniel Clamp."

"Well, no, not in person but—just look at this building." He waved his right arm expansively. "You know what kind of tenants they have here? There's a research laboratory upstairs—genetic research. Fooling around with animals, cutting them up . . . last weekend they took out a patent on a new kind of gerbil. People think *I'm* creepy."

"Well—I wanted to get away from Kingston Falls." Billy looked around them as they walked out into the large mall. The glass of the atrium walls glittered above them, the lunch hour crowd jammed the lines of different foodstalls. "I guess I did."

They got into the line at the McClamp King Burger stand.

"You got that right, kid. Have you heard these voices they have here now? Don't look at me like that. You know that white noise they play all the time?" He waved distractedly at the semi-hidden speakers pumping it out. "The static?"

"Yeah. That's so they can put people close together and they won't overhear each other. You're not supposed to notice it."

"Sure. But if you *listen* to it—there are little voices in there. You can almost hear what they're saying, but not really. *That's* a horror movie—THE BUILDING THAT WOULDN'T SHUT UP!"

"What would they do that for?" said Billy as he eyed the menu doubtfully. Clamp Crispies? He was afraid to ask what *they* were.

"That's what the world's coming to, kid. You can't even talk to yourself without somebody interrupting."

Billy laughed.

"I'm not kidding. Do you think I'm kidding. I'm tellin' you, I've got a theory. When there's too much order in the world, when it gets too much like a machine, clockwork—too much like this crazy Clamp Office Center—human nature rebels. Hell, maybe its the very cosmos that rebels! Cause, Billy, the key thing to remember about life is you gotta have balance—" He turned to the bright smiling waitress and ordered a Big Clamp, Clamp Crispies and a Clampa-cola.

"The same," said Billy, risking the Crispies as much out of curiosity as anything.

"Balance, Billy. Order and chaos. Too much order, and chaos is gonna come up and kick you in the butt."

"Grandpa Fred, Vampire Philosopher, huh?"

"You bet. But I'm not finished. You know, back in the old days, they used to have special crazy days when people got their ya yas out. We're talking the lower classes. Men dressed up as women. Women dressed up as kings. People pranced around in the street like loonies. And it was good for 'em, kinda let go of steam, you know?"

He leaned over confidentially and tapped Billy's chest with a gentle but firm forefinger.

"Look around you, Billy boy. Don't you feel the steam building up here?"

"Uh, well—" said Billy.

"Well, let me tell you, I do, and I feel it here!" He tapped his head. "Something's gonna blow soon, and it ain't going be Grandpa Fred."

Two trays of paper-wrapped burgers and side orders were pushed out in front of them.

They carried them to tables and chairs held up by huge metal C-Clamps.

"So what do you say, Billy?"

Billy didn't say anything at first. He was thinking about Kingston Falls. Billy had faced

chaos unlike Grandpa Fred had ever witnessed.

He sure didn't want to see its likeness again.

"Could be, Fred." He changed the subject.
Let's eat."

The "Clamp Crispies" proved to be a com-
bination of french fries and onion rings, all
shaped like the letter C.

Chapter
Five

If the Clamp Center could be said to have a heart, then that heart was the great man himself, Daniel Clamp. For it was his vision, his dreams, his entrepreneurship, his greed and most of all his money that had built the place.

However, if it had a brain, then it was down deep in the foundations of the huge building in its "nerve center." This was the nexus of electronic activity of the Clamp Center, monitored by technicians and a bank of computers worthy of the deck of Captain Kirk's U.S.S. ENTERPRISE.

Indeed with all the monitors it looked like the inside of a demented electronics store. Technicians hunched over meters, monitors and switches, tracking the building's systems like air traffic controllers track planes. In these monitors, various sections of the Clamp Center were revealed thanks to judiciously placed spy cameras.

High tech, plus lunch time smells of pastrami with mustard on rye.

Into the dark subterranean electronic caverns moved Frank Forster, dark and sleek, like a shark sliding into its lair. He swam past the technicians and the monitors, his nose twitching at the pastrami, but not going in for the kill.

There was fresher, bloodier meat around.

Frank Forster moved up to a man standing at the bank of controls. One panel of knobs was labeled WHITE NOISE and another VOICE.

Forster did not even bother to make a prefatory nod to the technician. "Let me hear the voices," he ordered.

The technician's hands danced over the controls. Voices came up on the speaker. They sounded like voice-overs on slick TV commercials.

They were, in fact, subliminal messages buried in the white noise mix, psychological tools to help create a smoothly functioning group of workers and consumers in a smoothly functioning Clamp Center.

"I'm an honest kind of guy—and not stealing office supplies works for me and the way I live today," stated one dynamic male voice.

On its heels followed a woman's voice suggestively cooing, "When I save money for the Clamp organization, I feel good about my-self *all over!*"

Followed by a cultured voice. "You know, I've been thinking—Mister Clamp would make a great president."

Frank Forster smiled. "That's fine." Forster turned to look out on the little sea of technology.

All was functioning smoothly, efficiently, just the way Forster liked it.

Forster wished people, even whole *societies*, could run smoothly and as efficiently as machines. Now *there* was a worthy goal for human evolution!

A technician tapped him on his arm, bringing him out of his reverie. "It's a call for you, sir."

Forster turned and saw that the technician was pointing up at a monitor. There, in all its blandness, was the face of Daniel Clamp.

Frank Forster did not have to come to attention; he was *always* at attention.

"Yes, Mr. Clamp," he said.

"I'm going to a meeting about the Vermont thing. It looks like that takeover is going to happen."

"That's terrific, sir."

"No kidding. How many guys do you know that have their own *state*? Did I show you that picture of the mountains?"

"Yes sir!" said Forster. "Tall!"

"While I'm in there, get that revolving door fixed downstairs. It shorted out last night while I had some money people here. Mrs. Tanaka is still spinning."

Forster flinched. Every glitch in His System was like a thorn in his side. "Yes sir. I'll—"

But Daniel Clamp was already gone, replaced by the Clamp Logo.

Forster was hurled into a snit. He cast about for some way to vent his thoroughly foul mood.

He found it almost immediately.

On a monitor over a technician's shoulder a spy camera showed a stressed-out employee lighting a cigarette in a storeroom.

Forster gleefully reached over and stabbed a button. He hoisted a microphone to his thin-lipped mouth.

"That's an unauthorized break period, pal!" he barked into the mike. "You don't work here anymore."

The startled male employee jumped about a foot into the air. He looked around like a trapped animal.

He brought up the cigarette to his lips for another hit of nicotine. It looked, thought Forster, as though this bozo might be used to hearing strange voices from nowhere. Good riddance! "We have a problem communicating here?" barked Forster, tasting blood and finding it sweet. "You're gone. Clean out the desk. One hour. Thanks so much."

Forster put down the mike and moved on to look over the shoulder of another technician. The guy was turning up a switch marked OXYGEN.

"What are you doing?"

"There's not much air in the building, sir," said the technician, pointing at quivering needles in the meters.

Forster sniffed and mentally calculated costs on the calculator embedded in his brain. "At four o'clock, people go into a slump. Then we give them oxygen."

The technician, used to such a cold-hearted attitude, just shrugged. "Yes sir."

The oxygen knobs stayed where they were.

Frank Forster nodded with approval and then moved on, surveying his dominion. He looked out onto the bank of television screens and monitors, CRT screens, toggles, switches and above all the white coated technicians, fleshy robots at his beck and call.

And Frank Forster found it good.

Upstairs, an entire half-floor of the Clamp Center had been rented by a biotechnology company called Splice of Life, Inc.

Some people, including even Frank Forster, had been doubtful about allowing a genetics lab in the building. Daniel Clamp had nixed them all on the subject, however, openly courting the group.

There were rumors that, with the aid of DNA engineers, Clamp wanted to do to human beings what he had done with old black and white films: improve them.

An interoffice messenger named Lincoln Johnson entered the reception area of Splice of Life, Inc.

Linc Johnson didn't like going to the Splice offices much. It gave him the creeps. It looked, at first, like any New York office reception area, with potted plants, deep pile carpeting, fancy furniture, a pert and pretty secretary-receptionist poised like an ornament at her desk.

Only from beyond the reception area, you heard strange noises—*animal* noises.

Squeaking. Scurrying. Screeching. Howling. Scrapings. Groans. Thumps. And once, Linc had even heard a strangled scream! Yikes, it was enough to give a guy the willies!

Today, as he walked in, he noticed that the receptionist was not at her desk and an inner door was cracked open slightly. He couldn't help but peek in.

What Linc Johnson saw inside made his eyes open wide.

The lab beyond, where beakers bubbled and bunsen burners flamed, where computers bleeped and tubing shook, was so high tech it made the rest of the building look like a tenement in the South Bronx. Scientists in lab coats conferred among themselves, the odd gadgets surrounding them looking like something from an alien planet. Rabbits, rats, and monkeys poked their noses from the bars of their cages.

And there was something else now, something that made the goosebumps on Linc grow even larger.

A tune.

A singing tune, rising from among the melange of other noise like a flute soaring above the rest of a cacophonic symphony.

That tune was sad and in minor key, and it got to Linc, burying itself in his mind. Unconciously, he picked it up. He found himself whistling the tune, enjoying the way the melody slipped through his lips.

"Can I help you?"

Linc's reverie was broken by the appearance of Peggy the receptionist walking briskly towards where he stood in the open doorway.

Linc gestured with his package. "Yeah, I got a delivery here . . ."

Peggy closed the door of the lab behind her and led him back to the desk to sign the receipt on his clipboard.

"What kind of stuff do they do in there, anyway?" asked Linc.

"We're not supposed to talk about it."

"That's for Doctor Catheter."

"Yes, no problem. I'll sign for it."

Linc noticed that the petite brunette had a bad case of the sniffles. She pulled out a pink Kleenex tissue from its pack and honked her nose. Then she signed his clipboard and handed it back to him.

He tore off her copy of the receipt and handed it to her. "Okay, this copy's yours. Thanks."

Funny. That tune wouldn't leave his head. He just kept on whistling it as he left the Splice of Life offices. He was happy to get out there, though. This place scared the hell out of him!

* * *

Life could be pretty wonderful, thought Dr. Cushing Catheter, head scientist of Splice of Life, Inc. as he strolled back into the offices from his lunch break. Especially when you dissected it.

A spring in his lanky step, he bounded into the offices, ready for new biological adventures.

Analysis! Exploration! The true final frontier was not space, but the interstices of cells, the very warp and woof of intergenetic forces that made up the boundless mysteries of life!

"Doctor Catheter!" said Peggy sweetly piping up from behind the desk. "This just came in for you." She handed him the package.

He took it, eagerly.

"Oh, good. This might be my malaria..." He opened up the package, fumbled out a vial, and read the label. "No. This is just rabies. I *have* rabies. And I was supposed to get the flu in this week!"

"I think the flu is in back-order."

She took out a Kleenex and blew her nose.

Hmm, thought Catheter. Could be worthwhile. He held out his hand. "May I have that, Peggy?"

"Oh, uh—sure..." She handed it over obediently.

Catheter palmed the slimy thing with great interest and headed for the back office.

"Back order," he said, shaking his head. "All a man wants is some fresh germs..."

He opened the door and walked into his

own precious world of beakers and petri dishes, test-tubes and needles.

Ah! The smell of disease mingling with rubbing alcohol! The scent of life's strands splitting! Here was the very stuff of life. He lived for science! Analysis! Dissection!

Smiling, his eyes lit up with an inner glow, the Doctor traipsed past the cages, peering at the various variations on the themes of "rat" and "rabbit" and "monkey." The animals looked back at him, and for a moment Catheter had the uneasy feeling that he saw hatred in their eyes. He dismissed the idea immediately. No, surely it was love, for Dr. Catheter was doing so much *wonderful* things for their species! At the very least all the metal and plastic they were hooked up with made them fashion statements of their species!

Catheter surveyed his lab with pride, and noted with satisfaction that his assistant, Wally Murphy, was hard at work.

Wearing his usual bloodstained lab coat, Murphy was standing at his station peering through an elaborate electron microscope.

Dr. Catheter walked over as he noticed that the fluorescent lights at Wally's station were flickering.

"Hello, Wally," said Dr. Catheter. "Your lights are flickering again," he said, crisping up his British accent for the right tone of authority.

Wally looked up. His eyes blinked in precise synch with the flickering of the fluorescent bulbs. "Are they?"

Dr. Catheter turned to a table. Perched on its top was a collection of vegetable plants, attached to collecting tubes that fed into a central glass vial. "How are we doing on the vegetable medley plant, Wally? I talked to the Bird's-Eye people again. They're very excited."

Wally sighed, scratching his splotchy face, a long suffering researcher. "We came close yesterday, Doctor. But it rejected the pimento."

Dr. Catheter nodded. "You'll get it, Wally."

"I'm very pleased about this bat project, though..." said Wally, his expression lightening as he led Dr. Catheter toward a group of animal cages. "You know, in some parts of this world, there are millions of bats. They could make terrific messengers, like pigeons..."

"Yes, but they only come out at night."

"That's what we're working on sir," said Wally, obviously becoming more and more pleased at the prospect of showing off to his boss.

They arrived at a cage where a resting bat was hanging upside down. An intravenous tube sticking out the bat's flesh connected to a drip bottle, whose label bore a shining sun logo.

"This is a formula of vitamins, hormones and Moroccan sunblock lotion. Soon, these bats will be totally desensitized to bright light. Watch—"

Wally flipped a switch and a bright sunlamp shone on the bat. The little creature stretched luxuriously, warming itself in the rays, like a basking cat.

A smile tugged the corners of Catheter's mouth. "Very nice!" He was a tall man whose narrow features and crooked teeth made him look very much like the Dracula of Hammer horror films. His eyes lit with a creepy light as he leaned toward Wally now. "I believe some of them feed on.... *blood!*"

Wally almost jumped out of his sneakers. "Oh, uh—that's a different bat, Doctor. South American."

Dr. Catheter was disappointed. "Ah. Well, good work nonetheless, Wally."

As Catheter started to move on, another scientist approached Wally. "Wally, could you let me have some growth hormone? I'm a little short."

Catheter did not get the joke.

He went to the other side of the lab.

Other projects to supervise, other researchers to see!

Amongst more cages and tubings and a brisk smell of fur and droppings, stood two scientists, hard at work, one with his back to Catheter. They were both a little below median height.

"Hello Lewis," said Catheter to the man facing him.

"Hi, Doctor!" Lewis was a cheerful, smiling man who looked like a younger version of Art Buchwald, minus the cigar.

"How's that cloning work coming?"

Martin, the other scientist, turned around.

He, too, looked like Art Buchwald without the cigar.

"*Really* well, Doctor." they answered in unison.

The twins traded words in streams of thoughts as though they shared the same brain.

"Say Doctor! Look at this!"

"... I think you'll find this interesting!"

They walked on down the aisle, and for the first time Dr. Catheter consciously noticed the minor key melody hanging in the air. It had been obfuscated before by the usual sound of Wagner's RIDE OF THE VALKYRIE hammering in his brain.

On a lab table was a covered cage. Martin pulled off the cloth covering it.

Dr. Catheter raised his narrow, slanted eyebrows.

In the wire cage, looking up with the most intelligent expression that Catheter had ever seen on an animal before, was something that looked like a stuffed toy merchandiser's dream. It was an odd but cute little creature with delightfully long ears, a tiny button nose, an expressive little mouth and moist, doleful eyes. Its arm wore a black armband as though it were in mourning. But of course, Catheter realized, that was impossible. Must be some sort of identification tag from some other lab.

"Some sort of rodent, apparently ..." said Lewis.

"And it can't take bright light," said Martin.

"Watch this, Doctor!" said Lewis. He opened the door of the cage and then scooted a Sony portable CD boom box closer to it. He clicked it on and a hot dance tune snapped from the speakers.

The frown immediately left the creature's features and he jumped through the opening of the cage and started to dance playfully to the beat.

Catheter frowned. "Cute, isn't he?" He peered suspiciously at the creature. "That may be genetic..."

"...we're not sure yet."

When Catheter looked back to examine the creature, he saw that it was edging along the table, clearly trying to make a break for it.

"Not so fast, pal." As Martin snapped the music off, Catheter grabbed the thing before it could run away. It was soft and warm, like a heated plush toy. He pushed it brusquely back into its cage and then turned a frown toward his associates.

"What's wrong with you two? He almost made a break for it."

"Sorry sir," said Martin.

"How are you going to proceed with him?"

Lewis answered. "Cell sample tomorrow..."

"...tissue cultures Thursday," finished Martin.

"And then there's body structure, mused Catheter. He smiled. "And for that, my little friend, we'll just have to cut you."

Chapter
Six

Billy was too preoccupied to take much notice of the messenger who walked past his desk whistling a familiar tune. He was still upset over having been ordered to put trees in his sketch of the Clamp Corporation's Chinatown project when he knew that it was a lie. The developer was not planting any trees on *that* piece of valuable real estate. Billy did what he always did when he was troubled; he talked to Kate. He was trying to talk to Kate over the high-tech videophone on his desk, and it was skewing her image enough to make her look like one of Picasso's more abstract renderings of the female face.

"So then she says I have to draw in a bunch of—" he was trying to say to Kate.

Then the lights went out. One damned thing after another!

"My lights went out!" he told Kate.

Over the phone, Kate said, "Jump around."

"What?"

"You sat still for too long. The building thinks you left. It's saving energy. Jump around."

Billy shrugged. He stood up from his chair and jumped to the left, then to the right.

The lights went back on ... but the vibrations of his jumping made the phone go dead.

"Nothing works here," said Billy with great exasperation. He reached down to redial, but at that moment the messenger passed by again, this time closer, and Billy heard his whistling loud and clear.

All at once, Billy recognized the tune.

It was as though someone had thrown a bucket of cold water over him and then given him a high-voltage hot foot.

It was Gizmo's song.

Gizmo's sad, wistful, beautiful melody!

He swept around and grabbed the guy who was whistling it by his shirt sleeve. "Where did you hear that?"

"Huh?"

"That music. Where did you hear it?"

"Oh uh—" The messenger guy hummed the tune this time. "Like that, right? Isn't that by Sting?"

"No it's not by Sting." Billy was dogged and insistent. "Think. Where did you ..."

The guy's eyes lit up. "Oh, hey, I know. I

was up in that laboratory, you know, on eighteen, and somebody was, like, humming it."

"Did you see who it was?"

"Nuh-uh, it was in the back—"

Gizmo was here!

Gizmo the Mogwai!

But in Splice-of-Life? Billy had heard absolutely dreadful stories about that place, stories of screaming animals, and maniacal, mad-scientist laughter issuing from behind locked doors, stories so terrifying they could make you lose the ability to speak simple phrases or eat solid food.

Leaving the astonished messenger behind, Billy Peltzer took off for the offices of Splice of Life, hoping against hope that he was in time, that he could rescue Gizmo before anything happened to his dear, good friend.

He'd figured the scam on the way up.

Billy Peltzer strode into the reception area of Splice-of-Life, lugging a box of tools he swiped along the way.

"How ya doin'," he said blithely to the secretary/receptionist at the front desk. "I hear your copier's down?"

"It is?"

"Oh yeah! Some guy called. Where is it?"

The bemused receptionist pointed. "It's back there."

She was pointing to beyond the door to the lab point. Billy tipped an imaginary hat and hurried on in.

He was immediately assaulted by the smell

of lab animals, mixed with the overpowering stench of chemicals. He noticed the ranks of lab equipment, then the cages housing the animals and his heart immediately went out to the poor living experiments. The worst of it was that Gizmo was here. You could sense the fear that permeated the air here. And part of that fear, part of that terror could belong to Gizmo.

Concentrating on his ruse, Billy hefted the toolbox over to the Xerox machine, pried open a side panel and peered inside. He pulled out a screwdriver and tried to make like a repairman.

As he "worked," he tuned into the conversation of two of the lab technicians. They were twins, he realized and both looked like Art Buchwald without the cigar! One was holding up one of the huge white rats that scientists always used in labs by the gross. The other was injecting a piece of cheese with a hypodermic needle labeled with a lightning insignia.

Another, apparently senior, scientist moved among them, watching what they were doing.

One of the junior mad scientists said, "This is the most interesting bio-electrical work I've ever been involved in. Here you go, boy . . ."

He fed a bit of the innoculated cheese to the rat.

"Think of it. . . . millions of rats in New York, and everyone hates them . . ."

"But if one of them could power a portable radio for a month . . ."

One touched the base of a light bulb to the rat's fur.

The bulb glowed weakly. The thin, older scientist touched the animal. An electrical spark jumped to his finger. He pulled it back, shocked but clearly happy. "Definite progress, fellows. If we could just make it safe to touch them . . ."

Good grief! What were these guys *doing*?

There was no time to waste. If Gizmo the Mogwai was here, he had to find the poor guy before these bozos got ahold of him.

Just then Billy heard—very faintly—Gizmo's song. Gizmo *was* here.

Billy moved back, following the trail of Gizmo's voice. It got stronger the farther back he got among the cages. Billy answered it with a whistle. He lifted the cover of one cage and jumped back in shock. Inside was a huge, hairy spider.

He moved on, searching, and monkeys chattered at him as he passed.

Gizmo's singing became stronger, and in a major key now. Gizmo knew that Billy was here!

It came from that covered cage there. As Billy moved closer he saw an array of sharp gleaming scalpels and other surgical instruments on a felt cloth by the cage.

What were they going to do to Gizmo!

Instantly, Billy Peltzer knew what he had to do. He turned around and started back in the direction he had come, only this time as he passed the chattering monkeys, he unlatched their cages.

Instantly, each monkey scurried to freedom.

A mass of them tore down the aisle, knocking over beakers and vials as they went, creating total pandemonium in their wake.

Billy quickly squatted back at the Xerox machine and looked up, surprised and innocent.

"Theodore!" cried one of the Buchwald clones as he looked down at a scampering spider monkey. "What are you doing out?"

"Alvin!" yelled the other. "Put down that DNA!"

They chased after the monkeys, adding to the confusion.

Billy hurried back to Gizmo's cage. He grabbed Gizmo, stuffed him into the toolbox, and hurried out of the lab.

He ducked into a men's room and leaned against a tiled wall, pulling in quick breaths.

Then he lifted the toolbox onto the sink and opened it.

"Gizmo!" he said, his heart filling with a torrent of emotion he felt for his furry little friend as he rembered all that they had been through together.

It was clear from his melting expression that Gizmo felt exactly the same. A boy and his Mogwai!

"Hey guy . . . did you miss me?" Billy asked, teasingly.

Gizmo tried to act coy, rolling his moist, so-alive eyes and shyly hedging away, doing a little soft shoe of reserve. But suddenly he turned full to Billy and simply fell, open armed, into Billy's embrace.

"Billll......eeeeeeeeee!" Gizmo squeaked with joy and delight.

Billy chuckled. "Yeah, me too." He put Gizmo up on a towel shelf. "Let's put you up here. We don't want to get any water on you."

Gizmo's twittering indicated total agreement.

"Gizmo, what were those guys doing with you?"

The look that washed over Gizmo's face was one of complete terror.

Billy cringed. "That bad, huh? How did you get in there? What happened to Mister Wing?"

Gizmo gave him a forlorn look. Mournfully, he pointed a petite finger at the black arm band.

Poor Mister Wing must have passed away, thought Billy. But then, he was a very, very old man, and we all had to come to our time eventually. "Oh, I'm sorry. But then—"

The sound of approaching footsteps interrupted him. Voices echoed from the anteroom between the bathroom and the hall.

"Quick—get back in here!"

Gizmo didn't seem particularly eager to get back into the toolbox but Billy grabbed him and stuffed him in. Gizmo twittered in objection.

"Shhhhh! Just wait a minute...."

He shoved the toolbox aside, and then

turned on a faucet and furiously washed his hands.

He heard someone's shoes click behind him, and an overbearing presence neared. Nervously, he turned around, slopping a liberal amount of water out of the sink and onto the man's shiny black shoes.

It was Mister Forster, with a glower on his mug that would freeze lava at twenty feet.

"You're wetting my shoes, Peltzer," he said.

Oh no! Hastily, Billy ripped a paper towel from its place and started to dive down to dry off Forster's shoes. "I'm sorry, sir. Let me—"

"Stand up, Peltzer. Come with me."

Billy grabbed the toolbox and followed Forster to the anteroom, where one of Forster's assistants waited holding a clip board.

Forster pointed to the sign on the bathroom door. "Do you know what that sign means, Peltzer?"

The sign showed a picture of a man.

"It means 'men's bathroom'."

"What is the man holding?"

"In the bathroom?"

"No, you idiot! On the sign!"

Billy peered closer. Oh yes, he hadn't noted. The man seemed to be holding a—

"Oh. A little briefcase, sir."

"That's right. Because this is the *executive* washroom. I don't think you belong in there, do you, Peltzer?"

"Oh, well. My mistake."

Forster pulled out his leatherette folder, took out the bar-code reader and ran the end over Billy's chest insignia again. He pushed a button and a paper tape readout churned out. Forster ripped it out and looked down at it.

"Lateness infractions," he read. "More washroom violations...and my goodness, look at those SAT scores!

Billy craned his head. "They're in there!"

Forster snapped the folder shut.

In Billy's hands, the toolbox rattled.

"What's in the box, Peltzer?"

"Well, as a matter of fact, it's art supplies." He rattled the box harder, hoping that Gizmo would get the message. "I'm mixing paints."

"I hope those aren't Clamp paints, Mister!"

"Uh, no sir...I bought it from the Arts and Crafts store down in the mall. You want to see the receipt?

Forster stared at him hard, and for a moment Billy thought he was going to call his bluff.

"Very well, but in the future be more mindful of the rules, Mr. Peltzer."

"Yes sir." Billy backed away, then headed down the hall eager to get away.

Forster watched Billy go, then turned to his flunky.

"Hmm. I think, Reynolds, our 'random' drug search later on should be very interesting...."

The assistant jotted down notes on his clipboard. "Got it, sir."

Forster smiled. Get *him*, he thought.

Chapter Seven

Back at his cubicle Billy Peltzer hurriedly slipped the toolbox under his desk. Looking around first to make sure no one was watching, he then put his hand in and hurriedly transferred the unhappy Mogwai to a drawer of his desk.

"Gizmo, you've got to be quiet. You don't want to go back to that laboratory, do you?"

Gizmo sighed and murmured a reluctant acquiescence.

"We'll go home soon and—"

There was a sharp gasp from behind him.

His nerves just about shot, feeling totally paranoid, Billy slammed the drawer and looked up.

Everyone's attention was directly down the

aisle toward where a bustle of activity cla-
mored down the hall.

Like heralds before a king, two bodyguards
muscled into the area, the vanguard for Oz
himself.

Striding down the carpet was none other
than Daniel Clamp.

He moved easily in his Bironi suit. The
scent of expensive men's cologne and money
advanced before him. The famous chin jutted
imperiously below a tight self-confident smile
and demeanor.

Clamp's head swiveled around, inspecting
the office area much as a captain inspects his
ship.

God, thought Billy. He was looking this
way! Was he coming to talk to him? Was he
coming, he thought in total paranoia, to take
Gizmo back?

But before Clamp could get anywhere near,
Marla rushed out to greet her commander-in-
chief, the boss of all bosses.

She was all flashing teeth and coos. "Mister
Clamp—sir. I'm Marla Bloodstone." Marla
Bloodstone radiated respect, shined of sych-
ophancy. "I'm the department head here. If
there's anything I can—"

Clamp's eyes simply skipped over her,
barely noticing the fawning woman. "That's
okay." He turned to the people in general.
"Everybody just relax and go back to what
you'd be doing normally. I know I haven't
been down here before, but that's going to
change. I'm going to be a little more 'hands-

on' with these operations from now on—"

As if to demonstrate Clamp looked around the offices, his eyes fastening on something in Billy's cubicle. "Hey! This is excellent!"

He was looking at the Chinatown drawing!

Billy looked back at the drawing even as Daniel Clamp drew close. "This?"

Clamp studied the picture for a split-second. "Yes. You've captured the whole essence of the project here. Look at the kids with the kites. That's warmth. I like warmth. What's your name?"

"Peltzer. Billy—*Bill* Peltzer."

Marla, saucer-eyed, looked on with mingled pride and envy as Clamp's hand moved out like that of Michelangelo's God, to shake Billy's hand.

"That's what we need here." He looked back to Marla specifically as though to say, "This is my Son, in whom I am well pleased!"

"People who produce!" He pointed to the drawing. "Let's lose those elm trees, though. People think 'elm,' they think 'Dutch,' 'disease'—"

The desk drawer rattled.

It was opening! Gizmo!

Billy hastily closed it.

"What's with that drawer?" said Clamp.

"Oh, it's uh...it's automatic," Billy explained. "It opens up now and then, in case you need anything."

"Huh? I didn't know about that one."

Clamp nodded and he moved on. The audience with Billy's department was over.

Marla moved up, a new appreciation for Billy Peltzer glowing in her eyes. "Did you hear that? 'People who produce' I've been working her six years and I've never even seen him in person."

"Well," said Billy. "He likes the drawing."

"This is big, Billy. This is a career opportunity advancement window." She paused and fixed him with a look. "For both of us."

"It is?"

"Clearly. We can talk about it at dinner!"

"Oh. That sounds great. I could do it, let's see."

"Tonight." Marla pronounced assertively.

"No, I can't tonight. I've got—" What he had was, of course, was Gizmo. To say nothing of Kate. "An appointment."

"I've got something tonight too, Billy. A brochure for the Clamp Cable Archery Channel. It's a total suicide trauma red alert deadline situation. And you know what? I'm letting it go to have dinner with you."

"I just don't think I can—"

The door rattled again.

"What's with that drawer, Billy?" asked Marla. "I know every feature in this building. We don't have anything that opens itself."

"Oh . . . I knocked against it with my leg. I was—"

"Billy are you keeping some kind of pet in there? It's a good thing Mister Clamp liked you so much, because—"

"A pet? No, no, I'm allergic—"

Marla put on some of the old insistent bitch

into her voice. "Let me see. Come on."

"You know—I think if we leave right now, I could go to dinner. Just a quick one—"

"Great." Marla's mascaraed eyes flashed enthusiastically. "There's this very chic new restaurant. It's Canadian. They clean the fish right at the table."

"Sounds terrific," Billy lied.

"Let me just grab my coat and I'll be right back."

She zoomed off, all atwitter at the prospect of having dinner with someone so tight and close with the Big Boss.

Billy waited to make sure she was out of radar range, and then he sat down at his desk again, and opened the drawer.

"Gizmo," he said into it, "I have to go now. Just wait here, okay? Just stay put for a few minutes and—"

He heard the click of high heels, smelled the cloud of Poison perfume, heralding Marla's return.

He closed the drawer.

"Okay!" he said in an overly bright manner. "Let's do it." He grabbed his sportcoat and followed Marla toward the elevator.

On the ride down, Marla stood uncomfortably close to him, as though sucking up the residue of the charisma shed from Daniel Clamp. "It's like just a fire alarm ambulance emergency room job I have, Billy. Twenty five and a half hours a day. Nine days a week, and I have the personal life of slug hermit-crab hibernating bear. I can't tell you how much it means to me to grab and share some quality time with a co-worker.''

Billy's heart was pumping like a locomotive. He was confused. Was Marla coming on to him? Or was this what they called *networking*? Billy wanted to do the right thing and advance his career. But if this was the right thing why did he feel vaguely guilty?

Kate. Right. He had to talk to Kate. Like right away, to explain. He couldn't let this opportunity go.

As the elevator reached the lobby and the doors opened, he turned to Marla. ''Could you excuse me for a moment? I'll be right back.''

''Sure.''

Billy hurried down the hall. Talk about everything at once! First, Gizmo and now this important dinner with Marla. He'd just have to get Kate to deal with Gizmo.

At one end of the lobby was a small office where the tour guides parked their stuff and punched their time-clocks. Kate was there, as she told him she would be. She was taking off her microphone rig and generally winding down from a hard day's work.

''Hi!'' she said, brightening up immediately upon seeing him. ''I'm almost ready—''

''Hi. Listen, Kate—''

The smile dropped.

''What's wrong.''

''Nothing...Um, nothing's wrong, but I can't go out tonight. I have a meeting. With some people.''

''Oh damn!''

"I know. I'm sorry. But it's good for—what we were talking about, you know? Letting people know I'm there and everything?"

"In the middle of the night?"

"Oh yeah. One more thing. Kate, I need you to do something for me. Something kinda big."

"What?" Kate asked, her big brown eyes looking a little bit hurt.

"Gizmo's here."

"Gizmo! As in terror time in Kingston Falls! How'd he get here in the Clamp Center?"

"It's a long story. I'll explain it later. He's up in my desk drawer. You have to take him home."

"Take him *home!* Billy, this is nuts. If Gizmo pops out with gremlins again and those things start running around in New York City—"

"There won't be any gremlins, or any 'things.' Just remember the rules. Gizmo can't take bright light. Especially sunlight. It'll kill him. And you can't get water on him. And the most important thing—never feed him after midnight."

"Can't he just—I mean, go back where you found him."

There wasn't much time to get her do this. Billy grew impatient and insistent. "No! I have to go to this meeting. *Please!* I'll be home as soon as I can!"

Kate relented, sighing. "Okay. Let me take this stuff off and punch out, and then I'll go and get him."

Billy felt a great burden lifted from his shoulders. "Great thanks!"

He gave her a quick kiss and rushed off to rejoin Marla.

There she was, looking like the cat who ate the canary. She was giving him a smile he'd never seen before. It looked nice, but it made Billy a little nervous.

She slipped her arm under his and pulled him out of the building. Neither of them noticed Kate watching them from across the lobby.

Chapter Eight

Gizmo the Mogwai wanted out.

The desk drawer was terribly claustrophic and besides, the scientists hadn't fed Gizmo much, and boy, was he ever *hungry!*

Yep. He had to get outta here!

A Mogwai had to move! A Mogwai had to explore! A Mogwai had to *eat!*

Gizmo knew that he was high up off the ground, but it didn't take long to figure out a way to get down. He found a box of paper clips and with his dexterous little fingers, he fashioned a chain-link ladder.

He threw it out and the end clattered to the floor. Then he started climbing down the makeshift ladder. Safely down on the floor, he scampered off for cover, just in case there might be humans around here.

Safely tucked behind a desk, he peered out, his ears unfolding wide on the alert for danger. He heard nothing frightening.

Then he opened his nostrils fully. They twitched. Mogwai senses on the alert for food!

His nose found a trace of coffee, the remains of a pastrami sandwich and a half a jelly donut.

His little stomach growled as he ventured out cautiously.

A Mogwai had to eat!

More specifically, a Mogwai had to eat before midnight. After midnight—whew! Gizmo didn't even like to think about that! After midnight was disaster! Look at what happened last time it happened in Kingston Falls! He was happy to be back with his old friend Billy, but it had been the boy's carelessness that had been responsible for that catastrophe! That was why Mister Wing had to come and take him back.

Well, he just had to real careful to make sure he didn't get wet this time. This place looked pretty dry, so Gizmo figured his search for food was safe.

But even as he ventured out into the aisle, Gizmo heard noises. Wheels rattled and a human voice muttered as a janitor pushing a cart of cleaning supplies came into the office area. He rolled his cart along, picking up trash and dumping it into his bin, murmuring to himself.

Gizmo hid himself from the towering human. He wanted to avoid trouble.

The janitor halted his cart's progress and shuffled over to the water fountain for a drink. He leaned over the spigot and pushed the button, continuing his muttering.

All he managed was to splash himself in the face.

He swore and tried again. The water shot every which way. A long, arcing stream of it splashed near Gizmo.

The Mogwai shivered. His fur stood on end! WATER! He *had to stay away from water!*

Gizmo jumped and rolled back under Billy's desk.

But the janitor sent another arc of water up through the air, and it came down on the other side of Billy Peltzer's desk. It slammed into Billy's trumped-up sketch of Chinatown, washed across it, and began to drip towards the floor below.

Gizmo looked up, to see the water streaming down, straight for him!

He couldn't get away. It splashed down on him full force, totally drenching one portion of his back.

Oh, nooooooooooooooooooooooooooooooo!

The pain kicked in immediately. It was worse than before, like a whole avalanche of needles sticking him. Agony! Gizmo writhed on the floor, barely noticing that the janitor, through with his rounds and disgusted with the water fountain, was wheeling his cart out of the offices.

Gizmo could feel the Offspring forming on his back, like giant bubbling carbuncles.

And then with THWIPPING sounds, the Offspring sprung.

Two furballs shot from his back and landed in an open drawer of a nearby filing cabinet.

THWIP! The painful Mogwai replication continued. A third furball caromed off a drafting table and bounced into a wastebasket.

THWIIP! Another furball shot from Gizmo's body.

Recovered somewhat, Gizmo hoisted himself up on his hands and watched as this little Superball of fur zoomed around the room like the Roadrunner bouncing off the walls of a canyon.

Gizmo frowned.

Big trouble! He got to his feet and watched with disbelief and horror as four newborn Mogwai hands reached out of the filing cabinet drawer, gripping the top edge from inside.

Oh oh. Two new Mogwais.

They poked their adorable heads from the filing cabinet, peering about at this brave new world. One was big and dumb looking. The other was smaller but looked much more canny and conniving. He seemed to be ordering the bigger one around. They looked rather like the characters George and Lenny out of that Steinbeck novel, OF MICE AND MEN.

The wastebasket rolled and rocked. It fell over, spilling all the trash that the janitor had missed—and another new Mogwai. Only this one was still folded up, and he was on his head.

Gizmo, his pain subsiding, stared on in wonder.

This one looked like one of those characters from the Loony Tunes he watched whenever he could! What was his name. . . . Daffy Duck! Daffy the Mogwai!

The little guy's eyes were rolling about with absolute joy of being alive. He watched his own little hands unfold and gave a little whoop.

"WaHOOOO!" said Daffy.

Another trashbasket tipped over, and a jumble of office wastepaper was forcefully tossed out.

A Mogwai with an extremely bad attitude strutted out, his evil eyes surveying the office.

Yikes! And this wasn't even a Gremlin and it looked mean. The new Mogwai had a mohawk haircut above a grizzled face and Gizmo immediately thought of him as "Mohawk."

"Uh oh," said Gizmo as the Mogwai spotted him. Those black eyes glittered with a maliciousness born from deep evil. Mohawk moved in on him.

There seemed to be some kind of telepathic contact between Mohawk and George and Lenny, because the two Mogwais jumped down from the filing cabinet and joined their evil leader.

Daffy seemed too preoccupied doing daffy things to bother with closing in on Gizmo.

Mohawk moved in, leering at Gizmo and then spit in his eye.

Gizmo tried to run, but the trio grabbed him and held him fast.

Meanwhile, Daffy was going absolutely whacky with the wet paint from Billy's drenched painting. He was getting wet paw prints all over the place.

Behind Gizmo was a vent opening, covered by a metal grating. George pointed to it and whispered to Lenny, who nodded his dumb understanding. Lenny shouldered his way to the grating and yanked the forcefit grate from the wall. He clumsily bumped George with the grate and George slapped him.

Then Mohawk pounced. He grabbed Gizmo, and with George and Lenny's help, pushed him into the hole.

In short order, the grate was put back up.

Gizmo's fellow Mogwais laughed at him as he tried to push the grate back out and failed.

They called him all kinds of names in Mogwai hisses and snarls and then scooted away, sneering and full of themselves, grabbing Daffy and pulling him along with them for their mischevious hijinks.

Gizmo was absolutely miserable.

He should never have left the desk drawer!

He desperately went to the other side of the vent and looked out into the hallway.

The janitor's cart and feet moved past him.

Oh, dear, thought Gizmo the Mogwai. Billy was really going to be upset!

Chapter Nine

At the Canadian restaurant up on the West Side, Billy Peltzer was busy thinking about advancement in Clamp Enterprises and simultaneously worrying about how Kate was doing with Gizmo.

Kate liked Gizmo okay, but she really didn't *know* him like Billy did, so all this was a bit nervous-making.

Meanwhile, Marla yammered away at him a mile a minute, talking about this and that in the advertising department, but mostly absolutely gushing over the attention that Daniel Clamp had paid to Billy today as he'd breezed through the office.

The restaurant—Handsome Dick Manitoba's Place—was a strapping big place that had once held a Hunan restaurant but had been renovated in cedar veneer. Potted pine trees, moose heads, and waiters and waitresses in Canadian mounted police uniforms, gave it that special Canadian allure.

Needless to say, it was all the rage among the West Siders, who discovered they had a taste for flapjacks, moose steaks and "Huskie puddle" shooters, (pineapple and lemon juice mixed with Canadian whiskey—a dreadful concoction, but the sight of Yuppie's lifting their legs in the "Huskie salute" and then downing them was a common sight at "The 'Toba" bar.)

Marla and Billy ordered up their salads and steaks and then Marla took a sip of Canadian wine spritzer, grimaced, and leaned over toward her dinner companion, surveying him intently.

After a long study Marla said, "You know, Billy. I've come to a conclusion. And that conclusion is that you've got potential at Clamp. Real potential."

"Oh," said Billy, nervously. "Really?"

"Yes, I definitely think so." She gave him another hard assaying look. "But we're going to have to do something about your clothes."

"How come?"

"Because they don't give promotions to a jacket like that," she said, turning up her nose at his Sears special, a polyester holdover from Kingston Falls days.

"Kate picked this one out for me. She's got really good taste."

"Maybe for bargain basement finds, Billy

Boy. No. What you need is something that says young, creative, plugged-in, but underneath—stable. The right jacket can do that. And a haircut."

"Yeah, I've been meaning to—" Billy said, self-consiously brushing his hand through his tangled mop of hair.

"We'll do it this weekend."

Throughout their meal (very rare steaks) Marla nattered on about all the things she was going to help Billy with. Her specially ordered Jolt cola in a champagne glass kept her even more frenetic and animated than usual.

The flickering candlelight softened her usually hard and brittle face. Her eyes shone with what Billy hoped was a caffeine glaze.

"Did you always know you were going to be an artist?" she purred.

"Well," answered Billy, considering. "I always liked to draw. When I was little, with my crayons, I would do these comic strips and drawings of the teachers and stuff..."

"I had crayons too, Billy. And when I was four years old, I was using them to write memos to the other children. Even then, I knew."

"Huh! That's something." He sipped at his Great White North Canadian beer.

Marla reached out to touch Billy's hand across the table.

"Isn't this great? We're finally getting to know each other. You can't do that in an office."

Billy had to agree. "Well in there, everything's business—"

Marla's tongue slipped out and softened her lip gloss so that it gleamed in the Canadian candlelight.

"Right. Now, let's talk strategy. You realize, this changes everything—for you, me, the department—"

"What does?"

"Your relationship to Mister Clamp. Your access. I can see a future, Billy. I see more office space...embossed letterheads...I see us..." Her voice lowered from catlike to pantherlike. "I see us swallowing up the publicity department!"

"Wow." The image was too much.

"I'm being open with you, Billy. I haven't talked about these feelings with anyone."

"See, I usually don't pay too much attention to office politics and stuff. I have so much work to do on the illustrations—"

"You have talent, Billy, and that's wonderful. It's a God-given blessing situation. But even an artist has to have goals."

"Definitely. It's like I was saying to Kate. I said, honey you know for an artist—"

"I can help you reach those goals, Billy," Marla cut him off, leaning closer to him. Her perfume was dizzying. As she leaned closer she seemed all silk and sighs. Billy Peltzer never realized that business dinners could be so erotic.

"If we join forces!" Marla continued.

"Oh, we should definitely join—"

Quite abruptly, Billy realized that there was a foreign object in his lap. Startled he looked down and found that it was Marla's stockinged foot.

"—forces," he finished.

The sensations were so sudden and unexpected and her smile so knowing and erotic that for a full few seconds, Billy could not speak further.

As for Marla, she did not, for a change, have to say another thing.

Her beaming face said—and promised—it all.

Fortunately, the Royal Canadian Mounted Police came to the rescue. Or so Billy thought for a confused moment, until he realized that it was a waiter standing by him. He looked up and was so shocked to find himself face to face with the large moose head the waiter carried that he spilled his beer in his lap, soaking Marla's foot.

Marla grimaced and pulled her foot away.

Billy, embarrassed and flushed beyond belief grabbed a napkin and dabbed at the spill.

"You okay there, sir? Another beer there, eh?" solicited the ever-helpful waiter.

"No, uh thanks. Everything's fine."

The waiter indicated the spectacular treat proffered before them. "This is a favorite Canadian dessert, sir. The chocolate moose. Can I cut you an antler there?"

"No thanks, I, uh—" He shot Marla an apologetic look. "I've really got to get going. I've

that appointment I mentioned, Marla.... I'm
sorry about your uh—"

Marla, back in control gave him her best
practiced smile. "Oh, that's okay, Billy."

Billy got up, but before he could go anywhere, Marla reached over and grabbed his
knit tie, pulled him down close to her and she
planted a kiss on his cheek. Billy slipped
loose and found himself confronted with the
chocolate moose once again.

"See you tomorrow!" breathed Marla as
Billy made good his escape, past the bemused
waiter.

"Good. Right!"

And, so saying, Billy Peltzer fled off into
the New York night.

Chapter
Ten

Kate Berringer was nervous as she left the elevator on the floor of the Clamp Enterprises advertising division.

She was quite ambivalent about seeing Gizmo again. Especially in New York City. Kingston Falls had been bad enough!

How could she ever forget how it had been, as a waitress for hordes of boozing, smoking, carousing, terrorist gremlins wreaking havoc on the tavern where she'd worked. All the stuff she'd gone through, thanks to Gizmo, was enough to give a girl gray hair at a tender age.

It had taken Kate awhile to recover from that whole nasty business. True, the end of it all found her in the arms of a wonderful guy, and ultimately it had all turned out for the best. But like Mr. Futterman you didn't escape from the experience of fighting lizard-skinned little monsters intent upon total destruction and chaos without a few mental and emotional scars.

She felt an extreme amount of trepidation as she moved toward the area that held Billy's desk.

She stopped short.

There were people there.

People—and something else. A dog. A big security dog, one of the monsters that lurked down in the building's basement. The rumor was that they roamed the halls at midnight, their food unwary burglars.

She stepped back into the shadows, hiding from them as the dogs sniffed the area by Billy's desk.

"Hah!" said a man's voice. "Good boy! I knew we'd find something in this guy's desk—"

Kate recognized him now. It was that awful Clamp assistant, Frank Forster. Hatchet man, with a hatchet face to match. He was flashing a light across Billy's desk and the Chinatown painting.

"Look at this mess! What kind of footprints are these!"

"Hard to say, sir," said the guard. "A possible gerbil?"

Oh dear, thought Kate. Gizmo!

"He's bringing pets to work!" barked Forster. "I don't believe this guy."

They looked around a bit more, but could

find nothing, and the dog moved on. Kate waited a moment, and then struck out toward the desk area. Billy said that Gizmo was somewhere around here. He must be hiding, she thought, but where?

Even as she stepped out into the office area, she heard a wolf whistle from behind her. She spun around and found herself confronted by a metal filing cabinet hanging out of which was a Mogwai.

"Gizmo!" said Kate in a scolding but fond tone. "How'd you get up there?"

The Mogwai's eyes rolled and he flopped around as though he had some sort of degenerative mental condition. He leered at her like Bugs Bunny on drugs.

She took him and he wiggled unpleasantly in her grasp. Gee, Gizmo had lost weight, too. Had Mister Wing not been feeding him?

"Billy said to take you home. You'd better stay in my purse till we get out of the building."

Hanging from her shoulder was her purse, and she was glad that she'd decided to bring in her big one today. She put the Mogwai inside it and carefully reslung it over her shoulder.

"Wahoo!" said the Mogwai softly.

That was funny, thought Kate, she didn't remember Gizmo ever saying "Wahoo!"

Downstairs, in the lobby, the last of the shoppers were doing their credit card things. Sensing food, the three new Mogwais—

George, Lenny, and Mohawk—had descended there rapidly, using the Clamp manual stairway.

They snuck up on the yogurt stand, ogling the dripping colored goo and the piles of delicious nuts, the chocolate syrup and candied fruit that people liked to pile on top of their treat.

The sight affected them all, but particularly Lenny. His tongue lolled, and Mogwai drool dribbled down to pool about his toes.

"Yum, yum!" he said, licking his chops.

Mohawk, however, was not concerned about things so petty as a yogurt stand.

His beady eyes traveled to a clock.

It was just past eleven o'clock P.M.

Mohawk grinned, showing pointy little teeth.

Almost time!

Up at her apartment off West End Avenue Kate pulled the Mogwai from her purse and set him on a countertop. Along the way home, she'd picked up some Kentucky Fried Chicken and the Mogwai was quivering with excitement at the smell of those special herbs and spices, to say nothing of the mashed potatoes and gravy and of course the cole slaw. He knocked over one of Billy's Dad's kitchen inventions, an Open-all—a device that can-opened, and bottle-opened while playing Yankee Doodle Dandee.

"Gizmo! Watch out, will you!"

The Mogwai's eyes rolled, his arms and legs thrashing around in excitement.

"Billy said to make sure and feed you before midnight."

She took down a plate and began to arrange some of the drumsticks on the plate along with the mashed potatoes and gravy and the cole slaw.

Ka - RASSHHHHHHH!

Kate jumped about a foot in the air. She wheeled around to find her blender in a dozen pieces on the kitchen floor, and the Mogwai wearing an "Uh-Oh" expression on the counter-top.

"Oh God. You have to be careful here, okay, Gizmo? We don't have the money to replace things."

The Mogwai nodded contritely.

Kate put the plate of food before him.

"Let's see if you'll eat this."

Daffy grabbed a chicken leg, opened his mouth wide, clamped down on the drumstick, and stripped off all the meat in one bite.

Tossing away the bare bone, the Mogwai dug into the mashed potatoes.

Unfortunately, he didn't like them.

He pitched the pawful he held, smearing half on Kate and half on the refrigerator.

"Euccch!" said Kate. "Gizmo—why?"

She got a paper towel and cleaned herself off, muttering, "I don't know what Billy sees in you!"

Daffy whooped, grabbed more chicken and

resumed chomping through the food like the Tasmanian devil on amphetamines.

Billy ducked into his dilapidated brownstone building, fumbled his key out, opened the door and then bounded up the stairs in record time.

He rang the bell.

"Yes?"

"It's me."

The sounds of the deadbolt issued through the thick door. The door opened and there was Kate, smeared with bits of food and looking profoundly unhappy.

"Hi. I'm sorry I'm late—" And then Billy noticed the full extent of the food fight damage. "What happened to you?"

Kate shook her head, fuming. But then she fixed her eyes off to the side of Billy's face. What was she looking at, Billy wondered.

"Did you have a good meeting?" she asked.

"Uh, yeah, it was fine." Billy missed the sarcasm in her voice. His eyes wandered the small apartment, searching for his Mogwai friend.

"Where's Gizmo?" he asked.

"It's in the kitchen. Billy—"

He struck off toward the small cubicle where the stove and refrigerator were. "Did you feed him?"

"Yes—"

"Hey, Giz, how are you—"

As he stepped into the kitchen he was almost struck full in the face by a slop of cole slaw. As it was, he got a spray of mayonnaise across the cheek. Billy could see a hairy arm sticking out from behind one of his Dad's crazy contraptions that he'd given Kate.

"What's going on Gizmo?"

Suddenly a little giggling form trundled out from its cover, and nailed Billy Peltzer on the forehead with a particularly greasy Col. Sanders biscuit.

"Yow! Gizmo, what's the—"

The creature's arms flailed like a windmill, and suddenly Billy's face was forcibly smeared with a glop of cherry cobbler desert.

Billy wiped it off and looked more closely.

The Mogwai sneered back at him. His eyes rolled and it pointed at him, yucking it up like one of the Three Stooges after successfully landing a pie in a face.

This wasn't Gizmo!

"Kate!" gasped Billy. "Kate, where did you get this guy!"

"In your office—near that drawer, where you said—" Kate's hand went to her open mouth. "Billy! Watch out!"

Too late. A single serving Jello pudding pack, swiped from the fridge blew up upon impact with Billy's chest, splattering him with brown chocolate mush.

"Hey, you little..." He advanced upon the goofy little thing accusingly. "Where's Gizmo? What did you do with Gizmo?"

The Mogwai spit and then tossed another pudding pack at Kate, who ducked just in time.

Billy looked up at the wall. The clock said, 11:15.

"We've got to get back to the Clamp Center!" said Billy to Kate.

"Billy. You said there weren't going to be those."

"There won't be. Not if they don't eat after midnight. He wished he could be as truly confident about that as he sounded.

Kate pointed at Daffy. "What about... him?"

"We'll have to take him with us."

He dodged another piece of food. Then he stalked forward and grabbed the alien Mogwai around the middle, almost getting bitten in the process. Billy stuffed the thing into his leather daypack he'd dropped on the couch in the living room.

The Mogwai squabbled semi-intelligibly words that sounded like "Wahoo! No! Elbow room! Don't fence me in!"

The bag jumped around wildly as Billy zipped it.

"You want to get out of there," said Billy. "You better relax."

The Mogwai settled down to a low rumble. "That's better."

Quickly, Kate slipped into her coat.

"Mister Wing was right," said Billy.

"About what?"

"When he came to take Gizmo back. I asked him how come he could understand what Gizmo was saying—he said you just had do know how to listen. But he said I wasn't ready yet. For the responsibility. And I'm not—"

As they reached the door, the buzzer sounded.

"Oh great!" said Billy.

"Who could it be this late?" wondered Kate.

"Only one way to find out," said Billy as he opened the door.

Standing there was none other than Murray Futterman—his narrow face twitching nervously. Being in the big city apparently aggravated his nervous tension. By his side was his wife, Sheila, looking a bit afutter too.

"Mister Futterman! Mrs. Futterman..."

"We thought you were coming tomorrow," said Billy, tucking the knapsack behind him so that the Mogwai's movements would not be too obvious.

"We thought so too," said Mr. Futterman. "The guys in my old Army outfit, they changed the date for the reunion. We tried to call you, but we had to get on the Greyhound."

"Thirty-two hours! We're sorry to come here so late."

"No, no," said Kate, ever the helpful hostess. "That's okay. Would you like some coffee, or—"

"No, don't you go to any trouble, hon," insisted Mrs. Futterman.

"Boy, we tried to get a cab up here." Mr. Futterman parked his luggage and coat on the couch. "Did you know they have Russian guys driving cabs in this burg? What if somebody gets in one of those cabs with a briefcase full of atomic secrets? Is anyone thinking about that?"

"Murray, you remember what Doctor Kaplan said. We're going to stay nice and calm." She turned to Billy. "Murray was a little ... distressed after, you know, what *happened* with those, um—" She mimed big ears and long teeth and nasty, nasty attitudes. In other words, Gremlins.

Mr. Futterman, of course, on top of his experiences in the war had been totally traumatized by the Gremlin rampage in Kingston Falls. The beasts had driven his tractor through the front of his house, and that had been almost too much. Only years of intensive therapy had put him back together enough to give him the emotional strength to make the journey to Manhattan for a very important date—a reunion of his air squadron.

Mr. Futterman had told Billy Gremlin stories from the old days claiming he had seen them in the war.

"Ah, I'm fine," said Mr. Futterman with a dismissive gesture. I was just a little jumpy for awhile—"

Billy's daypack squeaked. Billy slipped it under his arm and squeezed it to quiet the Mogwai inside.

"What's that?" said Murray Futterman, definitely jumpy again.

"It's okay, honey," said Sheila Futterman supportively. "I hear it too."

"Of course you hear it too. What do you mean?"

"It's uh—the plumbing here! Yeah! It . . . uh, makes noise sometimes!"

Sheila did a double-take and looked at both Billy and Kate with renewed understanding. She carefully scrutinized the side of Billy's face. "Oh, Murray—I think we interrupted these two."

Mr. Futterman said, "Huh?"

Then he seemed to spot the same thing on Billy's face.

Billy reached up, touched his cheek, examined the result on his fingertips.

Oh no! Lipstick! It must have been from where Marla kissed him as he was trying to get out of the restaurant. Her mark . . . Her brand!

"Oh, uh . . . that's from . . . my boss. I did some stuff that she liked. I mean, some work—"

He tried to catch Kate's eyes to show his true and thorough sincerity. But she pointedly avoided his entreaty for understanding.

"Uh, the thing is," Billy continued. "I'm afraid you guys can't stay here. I mean we'd love it if you could, but the, uh—the building's being—fumigated."

"Bugs, huh? Yeah, you can't be too careful these days. All kinds of weird bugs comin' into the country . . ."

Sheila said, "Oh. Well, that's okay, Billy—"

"Sure—we'll just book into a hotel."

"Really sorry . . . we'll call you . . ."

Billy, just as graciously as he could, showed the Futtermans to the door.

After their goodnights and plans for tomorrow's meetings were exchanged, Billy closed the door and then turned back to Kate.

She was staring cold daggers at the lipstick smear on his face.

"What . . . this?" He sputtered. "It was just one of those business things. You know, like—'Great job.' You don't believe me?"

"I believe you." Her face softened.

She *did* believe him.

"We better get going."

"Yeah," said Billy.

And, as quick as they could, they scooted down the stairs to catch a cab back to the Clamp Center before all hell and all heaven and everything between broke loose.

Chapter Eleven

The Yummy Yogurt stand at Clamp Center was typical of yogurt shops everywhere. Customers could have their lo-cal frozen treat covered with chocolate, syrups and candies and nuts until the final calorie total topped that of the daily intake of a Sumo wrestler in weight-gain training.

It was just the sort of place that could attract Mogwai. And, indeed, the terrible trio of George, Lenny and Mohawk had found it to their tremendous joy and glee.

Two young men were the yogurt jerks tonight. Mike and Eddie were teenagers from Queens, and this gig was their first regular job. They sported their bright white uniforms with pride.

Right now they were serving a final bunch

of customers. It was late, but one of the nice features of Daniel Clamp's mall was that it stayed open so late. People coming out of Broadway shows or clubs could go and do that one more bit of necessary shopping before they went home.

"Let me see," said Mike to a customer, standing over his his treasure trove of goodies. "So that's a Kona praline and banana-berry swirl with kiwis and peanut butter cups?"

"Yeah . . . or wait," said a woman, "are the peanut butter cups all natural?"

"I'm not sure . . . yo Eddie, are the peanut butter cups all natural?"

"I'm not sure." He turned to his co-worker. "Are the peanut butter cups all natural?"

"Gee . . . I don't know. Whaddya mean. They're Reeses, I think. So that's like the original peanut butter cups and like, that means they're natural, right?"

"I'm not sure. Aren't there additives in Reeses?"

"Aren't there additives in everything ma'am."

While the discussion raged, the Mogwais positioned themselves on the floor behind the counter to gobble up frozen yogurt running from an open tap.

"Yum," said Lenny, a gourmet apparently.

Eddie turned to get another dish of Very Berry mix, and saw with great consternation that the taps were on. But before he could turn them off, another customer was ragging him.

"Mister . . . I asked for Oreo cookies and

Gummy bears...this stuff." She held up a dish filled with wierd gunk. "Is like *hair!*"

"Ma'am, we don't have anything that's like—"

Both of their attentions were drawn at the same time to a motion from the topping bin.

A hairy paw was reaching out from below to scoop out a batch of M and M's.

"What is it?" shrieked the fat woman.

"It's a rat!" said the other.

"Yum!" said Lenny.

"What's going on here," said a man in glasses, looking cross and annoyed. "Did that woman say there are *rats!*"

"Um...no sir, she said there are *no* rats here!" said Mike.

It was into this rapidly growing pandemonium that Billy and Kate walked.

"Over there!" said Kate, pointing to the Yummy Yogurt stand. "There's something going on at the yogurt stand."

"Right!" said Billy, and they tore over to where the carnage was occurring. The scene had developed into a near riot as people were either running in to see the "rats" or running away from them.

"I'm telling you!" said a customer, eyes wide with horror and alarm. "There was a *thing* in the *trail mix!*"

"I don't just want a different yogurt, I want *damages!* " cried an outraged customer.

Billy grabbed the guy who'd seen the trail mix creature and pulled him around. "What kind of thing was in the trail mix?" he demanded.

"I don't know, a *furry* thing. And it's supposed to be *health* food!" The guy looked totally apoplectic.

Feeling a good deal of anxiety and apprehension, Billy checked the clock.

Twelve ten! A full *ten minutes* after midnight.

He pulled Kate aside.

"That's it. It's after midnight, and they've eaten. Now they'll make their cocoons...and if they get to water—"

"Come on," said Kate.

Billy could see his own fear reflected in her eyes.

She pulled him quickly toward the elevators.

"Where are we going?"

"Six floors underground!"

"Huh?"

"Look, I'm the tour guide. I *know* this building. I have to show you something."

The elevator door opened. It seemed like it took forever for the trip but only a few seconds passed. Kate led him out into a cavernlike floor, dimly lit. It smelled of water and concrete here. She pulled him along a catwalk, through an eerie half-light.

"It's along here," said Kate.

They almost ran smack into the things in the darkness.

Cocoons.

"What's *this*!" said Kate, horrified by the slimy humps.

"Oh, no! They've already made their cocoons!" Billy said, verging on panic.

"They're so . . . gross . . . !"

And indeed they were, slimy, glistening, green and already twitching and thumping about with inner life.

"The cocoons are gonna hatch by morning!" said Billy. "And if those guys get wet. . . ."

"Billy, I'm sorry I brought the wrong one home with me. But he looked like the—"

"It's my fault, leaving Gizmo alone like that. We've got to find him."

"Come on. This way!"

They came to a deep, square recess in the wall. Inside hulked massive machinery—pipes, pumps, meters—grinding with energy, surrounded by a chain-link fence.

"This is where the water comes into the building," said Kate.

"Great. Maybe if we shut it off, they'll even close the place down."

Billy went to a corner of the chain-link cage and started bending links back from the seam, trying to make a big enough opening to slip through.

Inside, the systems control center of the Clamp Center, one of the technicians, Henry Amos, got a beep from his terminal. The nighttime supervisor, Ned Marshall, hearing this little pinging sound, wandered over to have a look at the blinking red diagram displayed on the basement water machinery.

"Give me a video," ordered Marshall.

The technician typed a command and an image of a young man pulling back the links of the cage appeared on the screen.

"What!" said Ned Marshall. "Guards!" he shouted into a microphone.

He punched in a security alert.

Billy managed to open up a seam in the cage. He *had* to get in and turn off the water before the well-fed-after-midnight Mogwais could use it.

Suddenly, though, a bright light hit his eyes.

"Back off!" said a guard behind the light. "Put your hands up!"

He was waving a gun.

Billy's insides went watery. Guns frightened the spit out of him.

He moved away from the fence, Kate by his side.

The Mogwai in his bag chose that moment to move around.

"What's in the bag, pal?" demanded the guard.

"Nothing," said Billy.

"Oh yeah? Let's have a look."

"You don't want to," said Billy.

Ignoring him, the guard brusquely grabbed the bag, opened the zipper and looked down.

"Arggh!" he cried.

His head shot back.

Hanging onto his nose, teeth clamped tightly, was Daffy the Mogwai. The guard flailed his head around furiously, until Daffy was finally torn free, and flew away into the darkness.

"No!" cried Billy.

The pitter-patter of Daffy's departing footsteps echoed through the corridor.

The guard, recovered, grabbed Billy before he could chase after Daffy. He started handcuffing him.

"We have to find him!" said Billy. "Before he eats something!"

The guard pointed angrily at his nose. "He already ate something!"

Billy looked around for Kate—then he realized that she was hiding.

"Look," he told the guard. "We have to shut this building *down*. That thing that bit you—there are more of them, okay? And they're going to turn into—these *monsters* and—"

"Tell you what, pal. You can tell the cops all about these monsters, I'm sure they'll be very interested. . . ."

He started to haul Billy away.

"Listen!" said Billy. "I'm not crazy. People are going to be in a lot of danger. They wreck things. They kill people. If they get out of here, they'll destroy the whole city . . . they'll destroy *everything*. Listen to me—"

But of course the guard didn't. He'd probably heard this story before.

As he was dragged out of the basement, Billy heard the cocoons thwupping and gurgling and growing...

Growing.....!

Chapter
Twelve

Morning in New York City.

The sun reluctantly rose up out of the Atlantic, had its cup of coffee and a cheese danish at a Nedicks and then grumpily staggered up into the sky with its copy of the *Daily News* sports results.

At the Manhattan Midtown Precinct, Kate and Billy hurried down the steps past a group of handcuffed street mimes.

"Thanks for getting me out of there," said Billy. It had been his first night in jail, ever, and it had not been pleasant.

"It was easy," said Kate. "I just gave them next month's rent."

"When we get there—go to your job—like normal, okay. And just keep your eyes open. What time is it?"

Kate examined her watch. "Six thirty."

They hit the early morning streets in a run toward the Clamp Center.

The dawn's nicotine stained fingers grasped the Clamp Center as the first workers straggled in. The myriad shops in the mall made their opening ablutions and ministrations, rolling up chain fences and unlocking doors.

There was no sign of last night's yogurt melee. It wasn't even part of the building grapevine news this morning. Rats in Manhattan? So nu? Like finding New Jerseyans in Hoboken.

The newsstand was getting its bundles of TIMES and POSTs and DAILY NEWS to set up beside the porn magazines, Racing Forms, and stacks of, yes, the New Yorker. Corrugated metal security gates rose above the Really Wired espresso cafe, the Tippy Top Tanning Salon and Scissors Wizards, a trendy haircutting place.

Life was also stirring in the deepest, darkest bowels of the building.

The cocoons were opening up.

Smoke drifted eerily above them as the slimy things began to burst open, gushing great gouts of gangrenous goo as they released their hellish spawn.

Upstairs, Gizmo the Mogwai was lost.

He'd finally managed to get over his attack of fear and claustrophobia about an hour before, and he'd crawled up one narrow vent and down another, but he'd managed to get himself so terribly lost, he didn't know what to do.

Oh, Billy, Billy, he thought. Where are you? He inched forward farther into the darkness of the vents.

Suddenly, the floor just *disappeared* beneath him.

Gizmo fell down a long shaft, flailing his arms helplessly, grasping uselessly for purchase.

Down and down he fell, and he thought for certain that the end of the shaft would be the end for him. . . . and he would never see Billy again, never get to say goodbye . . .

The darkness turned into a murky, smoky half light—

And he landed in something soft and giving, cushioning his fall so that he came to no harm.

One of the Mogwai cocoons!

As he got up and backed away, Gizmo recognized it and its brethren for what they were. These things had once been George, Lenny and Mohawk!

He backed away, trembling with an overwhelming sense of impending doom.

"Bill—eeeeeee!" he squeaked.

He had to get away.

He had to get away and warn Billy.

He had to stop this insanity from happening . . . again.

If the gremlins got loose in New York City, Gizmo didn't even want to think about it. Suddenly, without warning, a green claw grabbed him from behind, jerking him backward, off his feet.

He was wheeled around and there, looming before him like the Creature from the Black Lagoon, all green and lizardy and big eared with scales and sharp fangs and evil luminous eyes was a huge Gremlin with a haircut straight from a James Fenimore Cooper novel.

Mohawk!

The noxious thing leered at him like the devil himself grabbed poor little Gizmo and shook him. The malicious gleam in his eye said all that needed to be said.

"I'm going to take care of business, you nerd you," the malicious gleam said. "You're going to get it you dumb little Mogwai."

The demonic Gremlin laughter of Mohawk's two companions reverberated behind the pair. Gizmo was backed against a wall right by a set of master controls for the building's electrical system.

Pinning Gizmo's little neck against the wall, Mohawk beckoned to his cronies. George and Lenny—grown into creatures out of Mephistopheles' nightmares—shuffled forward, green faces leering at some private obscene joke.

Quickly, the powerful Mohawk ripped loose cable from the wall and used it to tie Gizmo down.

He gestured toward Gizmo and looked at

the other two Gremlins in a sinister fashion as though saying, "He's all yours, guys. Enjoy!"

Then he moved off into the shadows, nefarious plans brewing in his mind.

George excitedly indicated the gridwork of the lighting-panel and tapped an exposed cable. Tongue lolling stupidly, dripping purplish saliva, Lenny advanced, grabbed the cable and yanked it free.

Sparks flew as Lenny handed George the frayed end of the live wire.

"Noooooooooooooooo!" screeched the Gremlin, but too late.

It gave him a shock that knocked him a full six feet away.

Picking his smoky self off the ground, George angrily stomped back, slapped Lenny roundly across the chops, and then grabbed the cable by its insulated end.

His gimlet eyes glittered as he held the end of the power cable out to touch the helpless Mogwai.

Billy Peltzer and Kate Berringer ran breathlessly in through the lobby doors of the Clamp Center. Most of the businesses were open now, and a sea of people washed through the mall area—all oblivious to the green menace brewing in their building.

"Billy," said Kate. "What if they're already..."

Billy, totally distraught but not giving up hope, "They are. Come on."

They were running past the newsstand when they ran into Grandpa Fred, dressed in his full Vampire regalia.

"Hello, Billy," said Fred. "The building's *completely* screwed up today."

Billy hurried on past the Caped One, pulling Kate along with him. "Hi, Fred. I know....."

Fred watched them go. "Sure. You're young. You know *everything!*"

They darted ahead to the newstand. Billy stopped there and grabbed four souvenir flashlights—each in the shape of the Clamp Center.

"Eighty-six thirty eight with tax," said the bored lady in charge.

Billy didn't hear. "I'm going to go up and—" he said to Kate.

Abruptly her words sank in.

"*How* much?"

The clerk shrugged. "Four times nineteen ninety five."

"Put it on my bill," said Billy.

He gave Kate two of the flashlights and then hurried her along through the lobby.

"Remember," he said. "They can't stand bright light. If one of them gets near you light him up."

Suddenly, out of nowhere, Marla swooped down on Billy. Before he could do or say anything at all in the way of objection, she gave him an intimate squeeze and a big kiss.

"Good morning, Billy," she said, breathlessly. "That was so nice last night. We're going to have to do that again—"

Billy, knowing he was in deep trouble, nonetheless tried to act as if nothing was wrong. He fumbled and stammered trying to make proper introductions.

"Uh—Marla, this is Kate, my—"

Marla pretended she hadn't seen Kate before. Now, glancing over, she gave Kate the once over and said, "Oops, I'd better get going. See you upstairs, Billy." She gave Kate a cold smile. "Cute hat."

Oh boy, thought Billy. I've got the devil to pay now. He turned to Kate and saw that she was steaming. "Uh, Kate—listen, I think I better explain—"

"Don't do any explaining right now, okay?" she said in a cool, measured voice. "I'm too mad."

A full blown lover's quarrel could have erupted here, but Billy was saved again, this time by the appearance of Kate's supervisor, a dour-looking spray-on brunette whose Clamp Center hat looked a little wilted.

"Kate—you're up, honey."

"Excuse me," said Kate, cutting off the discussion in mid-chill. "I have to go to work now."

Billy shook his head. He didn't have the luxury of worrying about the state of his relationship with Kate. At the rate things were going, this city was going to be destroyed before he and Kate had a chance to even start deteriorating. "But—look, I'm going up to

Systems Control. If I'm not back down here in fifteen minutes—"

Kate scowled at him. "Billy—if we all get through today alive, you're in *big* trouble!" She stalked off.

"Kate—" he started to plead, but she was already gone.

"Terrific!" said Billy, and headed for the elevator banks.

As he passed a clothing store, he noticed a teenaged girl holding up a pair of jeans.

"Excuse me," she asked a clerk, "do you have any styles that aren't, um, fringed?"

Billy looked. The jeans were shredded from the knees down. They weren't fringed, they were *clawed.*

The Gremlins were on the loose!

From within the store, Billy then heard a strange cry.

"*Wa-hooo!*"

A few minutes later, Billy Peltzer had found his way into the Clamp Center control headquarters nestled deep beneath the building.

Frank Forster was making his morning rounds.

Billy went up to him.

"Mister Forster—"

"Peltzer! What are you doing in this building? You got yourself arrested here last night and you come *back*!" He turned to a technician. "Get security up here. He's out."

Forster started to walk away, but Billy followed him.

"Mister Forster, we have to evacuate the building. Right now!"

"Oh, we do? Why's that?"

"There are.... creatures in the building. They start out as these small, furry animals, but then they eat and they go into cocoons and then they become small, green—"

Forster shook his head, astonished, then angry. "Drugs! This is drugs, it's got to be. You're on a groovy little trip aren't you, Peltzer? Well, let me tell you something, Mister Flower Child—"

"Just listen to me!"

A technician twirled around in his chair. "Wait a minute, this is good. They start out furry and then they have the cocoons....."

"First they eat..."

"Well sure," said another technician, joining in on the fun. "If you go into a cocoon, you want to have a little something to nosh."

More of the technicians joined in on the fun, laughing and joking.

"Oh no! We're all gonna get slimed!"

Chapter
Thirteen

Leading a tour group through the Clamp Center was no treat at the best of times but when you were worried about an imminent Gremlin infestation, as Kate Berringer was, it made things much more difficult.

She couldn't get the images of those gooey, smelly cocoons out of her mind...

Cocoons hatching and disgorging those... those awful things.

When she was tending bar at the tavern back in Kingston Falls, she'd served some pretty seriously weird characters but those Gremlins had been like intense parodies of all the sins of humanity. They sure had torn hell out of that tavern. Imagine what they would do to New York City!

Of course, there was always the possibility

that maybe even Gremlins wouldn't be able to deal with Manhattan.

Kate's tour group this morning included the usual crowd of Hawaiian-shirt garbed people from the hinterlands and European tourists in shorts, sandals, and white socks. Her lone Japanese tourist was a young man who had formally introduced himself. His name was Katsuji and before the tour started he'd presented her with a small package of Super Lemon candy with a sincere bow. She'd thought that was sweet, but as the tour progressed young Katsuji began to get on her nerves.

The guy was absolutely *freighted* with an arsenal of photography equipment. Dozens of cameras and lenses hung on him like high-tech ornaments on a Bonsai christmas tree. Among this assortment, was the latest Sony video camcorder, slung around his neck like a Star Wars laser weapon.

The problem was that he was so busy using this equipment to record the tour that he kept falling behind the group. Not only was losing tour group members frowned upon by the administration, but Kate was also supposed to complete the tour in an amount of time specified by one of the Clamp Corporation's efficiency experts.

By the third time Kate had halted the tour in order to chase after him, Kate was beginning to lose patience with Katsuji.

"Sir," said Kate, trying to stay pleasant and finding it very, very hard. "I'm sorry, but you have to keep up with the rest of tour group."

Katsuji paid no attention to Kate's scold. He merely focused his camcorder on her.

"Excellent! Thank you! Please give me some right profile as you continue speaking!"

Kate shook her head and gave up. She went to the front of the group again.

"As I was saying, these are the studios of the Clamp Cable Networks. Now, if you're all very quiet, we can go in here and watch a program being videotaped..."

She led her group into Studio C. Right now, they were taping "Microwave with Marge." It was not one of Clamp Studio's more sterling productions but this was the one studio they would let the tourists into.

The studio was your typical dark cave around a tacky set made bright and photogenic with expert lighting. Microwave Marge was gushing now over her latest creations as she set a tray of grayish canapes down beside a hot aromatic Vienna sausage casserole.

"Now, this week here on 'Microwave with Marge' is our special 'Salute to Luncheon Meats,' and I'm very excited about these recipes, so let's just jump in with some hors d'oeuvres. You know, these bologna and bean dip roll-ups are so easy when friends drop over, and if you want to make it a little extra special you can get some of these little sword-shaped toothpicks. You put these through the bologna and that's our 'Viva Zapata' appetizer. People are simply crazy about these—"

* * *

Downstairs in Clamp Center control headquarters, Forster waited impatiently while the
technicians quizzed Billy. The discussion had
become something like a Sunday school class
discussion of theology among doubting, wise-
acre kids.

"Okay, wait," said one technician, a guy in
something close to a crewcut. "What if one of
them eats something at eleven o'clock, but he
gets something stuck in his teeth—"

"Yeah, right, like a caraway seed"

"Whatever, right. And then after twelve
o'clock, it comes out—now, he didn't *eat* that
after midnight—"

"Look, I didn't make the rules," said Billy.
"There are—"

"The rules!" said Forster, shaking his head.
"I can't believe this!

"Or what about if he's eating in an airplane
and they cross the time zone!" suggested another and everyone started laughing at the lu-
dicrous thought.

Laughing, that was, until two big green
scaly arms burst out of the console, ripping
aside control buttons and speaker grilles in a
burst of sparks and smoke.

Oh God, thought Billy, too paralyzed with
fear to move immediately.

It's happening!

Clawed fingers closed around a technican's
throat and pulled him down to bash him
against the control board. A particularly ugly
and nasty Gremlin emerged.

A Gremlin wearing its multicolored hair mohawk style.

With an evil leer, the Mohawked Gremlin continued to choke his new victim.

"Help me!" the guy cried.

Forster took off, getting as much distance as possible between himself and the Gremlin.

Another technician went to his colleague's aid.

The Mohawked Gremlin slashed his arm with sharp fingernails and whooped with nasty glee.

Billy shined the flashlight in Mohawk's face. Screeching, the Gremlin raced away into the darkness for cover.

Forster and the technicians stared at one another with total bewilderment.

And then they looked at Billy Peltzer as though they'd just seen him for the very first time.

Microwave Marge stood in her jerrybuilt super-suburban kitchen set. A soup-pot rested on a kitchen stove and a match flared in Microwave Marge's hand.

"*This* is how we *used* to cook for big groups, before we had our microwave ovens and the other modern appliances. It would take *days* . . ." she turned on the gas and she lit the burner, "*days* to plan the menu and *absolute hours* over a hot, hot stove to do the cooking. But now, we can make this same tuna-noodle cheez-product chowder surprise in just a few minutes, and you can feed anything from a

high school reunion to a complete Georgia
chain gang with this kind of quantity."

She clopped the lid onto the mammoth
soup pot.

"Whew! Now, if we step over here...."

Suddenly, the lights flashed on and off.

Marge looked around, more annoyance on
her face than surprise. "Huh? Is this a brown-
out or something?"

From somewhere came a tap-tap-tapping.

Microwave Marge gazed around her. Wher-
ever was that noise coming from?

When she realized that it was coming from
the pot—now *that* was when Microwave
Marge became truly surprised.

This surprise was significantly com-
pounded when she reached over and opened
the gigantic soup pot.

A Gremlin stood up, trailing wilted celery
and strands of noodles, grinning goofily.

Even though he was now a Gremlin, the
thing could be recognized as something that
had once been Lenny the Mogwai. He looked
like a Gremlin gorilla after a lobotomy. He
whipped out a turkey baster and squirted Microwave Marge with it, sending soup all over
her face, her apron and her spanking clean
shirt.

"Argh!" cried Microwave Marge. "What is
it!"

Harsh, awful laughter sounded behind her.
She turned to find herself confronted with
another Gremlin: the former George the Mogwai, dressed in an apron and chef's cap, eyes

gleaming with anticipation at the prospect of fixing a lovely *lovely* dinner!

As Marge turned to the cameraman, waving wildly for some kind of assistance, George the Gremlin turned his evil eye upon the gigantic microwave oven in the very middle of the set.

And boy, was it a beauty!

A Japanese number, from a brand new outfit in Japan called NUKEIT, this baby was loaded with a gigawatt generator that crisped bacon the second it started a buzzin' and a hummin' away! Marge's pride and joy, it shone and sparkled, freshly cleaned with Clamp Detergent's Lemon-All Four-in-one Cleanser by her hands alone.

"Mi—cro—wave!" said George the Gremlin.

The Gremlin raced dementedly around the kitchen, grabbing metal pots and tossing them into the open door.

When the Nukeit microwave was chock full, the Gremlin slammed the door closed, tapped the controls onto FULL MAX and pressed the start button.

The Nukeit nuked it.

With a rattling hum, the microwave started beaming the metal pots.

As an expert on the subject, Microwave Marge knew well what happened when you put metal in a microwave oven. And lo and behold, here was lot and *lots* of metal in a very powerful microwave oven, turned up to full power.

"Look out!" said Marge.

For when microwaves hit metal, they arc.

And when there's lots and lots of metal they arc and arc a lot.

The microwave oven zapped and flashed with blue light. Arcs flung themselves hither and thither with incredible raging violence. The microwave oven rocked back and forth like the Brave Little Toaster that Could—but didn't.

It blew.

The set was showered with glass. People screamed and ran.

Seeing her precious microwave oven explode was too much for Microwave Marge.

"Let's get the hell outta here!" she said, grabbing her cameraman. She pulled him after her and they escaped together.

Flames licked up toward the ceiling from the havoc and the wreckage.

And the Gremlins cackled with totally evil glee.

Chapter Fourteen

Booms fell noisily. Gremlins mooned live cameras, beaming their green and knobby butts out throughout the astonished nation of America. Fortunately, though, the cameras were soon trashed and the transmission cut off, or doubtless thousands and thousands of Americans would either have gone mad or simply changed the channel.

Elsewhere in the building, equal pandemonium reigned.

For example, it certainly hovered like a fury around Gizmo the Mogwai.

One of the Gremlins had the poor guy scotch-taped down onto the top of a photocopy machine. The awful creature was busy taking copy after copy of the unfortunate Mogwai.

Indeed, it was none other than Mohawk, come back to commit sadistic havoc upon the helpless creature.

Back down in the Clamp Center Systems Control, the technicians were both somber and very, very rattled.

After all, it isn't every day that little green monsters invade a skyscraper.

They worked urgently at their consoles.

A panicked Forster paced behind them, from time to time glancing at their monitor screens with total disbelief.

"Mister Forster," said one to the boss. "I show lighting brownouts in five locations."

"I've got a climate control malfunction, floors fifteen and sixteen—"

"What the hell's going on," said Forster, raising his arms as though entreating Heaven itself

"Uh sir." He took a few steps and indicated a monitor. "The Pest Infestation Monitor..."

On the screen was an alarmingly rapid proliferation of dots, spreading over the building diagram.

Forster said, "What is that? That's not rats, is it."

"No sir, I'm afraid it's not—"

A videophone rang near Technician 3—he grabbed it.

"Systems control!" he barked into the phone.

Kate Berringer's face filled the videophone screen.

"Is Billy Peltzer there, please?"

"No," answered a technician. "He said he was going to Mister Clamp's office—hey do you know anything about—"

"Thank you."

Upstairs at the videophone, Kate Berringer hung up. She ran toward the elevator and got on.

"Thirty eight!" she demanded expecting the obnoxious but familiar voice to respond.

"Thirty eight, babe!" screeched a Gremlin voice in its place.

Horrified, Kate tried to get out, but the doors slammed shut in her face. And the elevator started moving...

—and then jerked to a sudden stop.

At the very tippy-top of the huge structure that is the Clamp Center resides a whole suite of offices insulated from the rest of the building by more than just distance and man-made materials.

It was here where the famous Daniel Clamp wheeled and dealed and generally operated his expansive and growing, growing GROWING empire with the glee of a little boy playing Monopoly by himself and cheating.

Daniel Clamp sat at his desk.

He was a tall, angular man. Some people said that he looked like a skinny Gary Cooper while others claimed he looked more like Jimmy Stewart after a couple years of working-out.

Daniel Clamp liked to say that he looked like a young Billy Graham who'd just found out that people weren't really going to hell after all, and that he could drink and womanize as much as he wanted and still get through those wondrous Pearly Gates.

Not that Daniel Clamp drank much. Or, for that matter, womanized. Hell no. Unlike his arch-rival, Donald Trump, he didn't really care to share his toys with anyone. The fact that he could do just about anything he wanted to—was enough to keep him happy for minutes at a time.

Daniel Clamp sat at his desk, looking out at the expanse of neatly placed office stuff atop the high-polished teak. All high-designer stuff, expensive as hell . . . and the funny thing was, Clamp was bored with it.

He sighed.

Daniel Clamp stood up from his desk.

He walked to the windows.

The freshly cleaned windows sparkled in the morning light and he looked out onto the skyline of Manhattan. His eyes darted from building to building to building.

Mine.

Mine.

MINE!

If the laws of real estate were "location, location, location" then right now Clamp Enterprises was "New York, New York, New York"—the city so nice they named it thrice!

The Trump era had the Big Apple, he was working on the Big Orange out west, and his encroaching takeovers were the talk of the financial world.

And to think it all started with a fifty thousand watt radio station in Peoria, Illinois, a disc jockey with dreams, an old Ford pick up truck—and an inheritance of a mere fifty million dollars' worth of real estate.

Ah, yes, thought Clamp looking out across the East River with vast satisfaction. Those had been the days!

Still, things in the office were getting a tad dull today.

No big takeovers due until next week.

No celebrity balls or sports events until this weekend.

His lunch with Liz Taylor at the Four Seasons wasn't until twelve-thirty.

And his date with this season's hot model wasn't until 8'clock tonight.

What was a poor bored billionaire to do?

Daniel Clamp pushed the button of his intercom.

"Miss Jones, have you shredded my mail from this morning?"

The voice came back promptly and efficiently from the pert and pretty secretary. "I'm just finishing, Mister Clamp."

"Good. Let's do some memos."

"Yes sir. Just a moment sir."

"Make it snappy, Miss Jones! I'm a busy, busy man."

"Yes sir."

What to do, what to do? The billionaire cast about.

His eyes were caught by something on the far wall. The entirety of this section had been set up like a gigantic television and radio control center, with monitors and such stretched out in banks. Screening now upon a monitor—and presumably being broadcast now upon one of Clamp's several cable stations—was the Frank Capra classic IT'S A WONDERFUL LIFE. Jimmy Stewart was running down the snow-covered street now, yelling "Merry Christmas, movie house! Merry Christmas, drugstore...!"

And it was an affront to Daniel Clamp's eyes.

It was in black and white.

What could be wrong!

Clamp scowled. He stalked over the banks of controls and looked down.

Relief flooded him. Oh, of course! Just a little glitch!

A smile of control and pleasure swept over his well-defined features as he reached over and turned a knob.

Computer-generated color washed over the black and white classic.

Clamp sighed with relief and pleasure. Clamp knew what the public wanted. Always did, always would.

The outer office fronting the huge interior of Clamp's sanctum sanctorum was manned, (or womaned, rather) by Linda Jones, a secretary of uncompromising efficiency, enormous breasts, pneumatic legs and the morals of an alley cat.

Needless to say, she was going far in Clamp Enterprises.

Just now she was pushing a letter through the shredder off to the right. It was a big shredder, absolutely the latest model.

The Ollie North Shredder it was called.

When Daniel Clamp's voice erupted over the intercom, she snapped to immediate attention, her blonde hair flouncing over her shoulders. She popped her bubble gum, then picked up her steno pad.

"Memo time."

"Yes sir." Pen poised to paper, she was ready.

Mr. Clamp didn't like to dictate to her in person because he got all confused trying to talk while she and her breasts were in the room.

"First one, to Frager in Public Relations. Let's have the people in Chinatown give a street festival as a spontaneous outpouring of appreciation for what I've done for their community..."

Miss Jones generally skipped breakfast to give herself more time for makeup application. She usually picked up a sandwich at the health food store downstairs for a mid-morning snack. Today it was peanut butter and banana sandwich.

Little did this vision of sexy secretariness realize it, but slinking beneath her desk was something far more nefarious than her silk stocking, and he had plans for that sandwich.

While she was busy taking down the memo

from Mister Clamp, the Gremlin (Mohawk, in fact) stood up behind her, opened her sandwich and stuck a cocked Acme mousetrap between the slices of bread.

Stifling a snigger, the Gremlin darted back under the desk and waited for the fun.

It was not long before it came.

Linda Jones got hungry and she reached for the sandwich.

She pulled it to her mouth and took just the biggest bite her petite mouth could manage.

SNAP!

Linda Jones screamed.

But when the little green monster jumped up from behind her desk—that was when she *really* screamed.

Inside his vast office domain, Daniel Clamp heard his secretary scream, a scream of pain and fear.

Daniel Clamp was many things, but he was no coward. A lesser man would have simply locked the door and dialed security, but Daniel Clamp was a pure American and he rushed to the aid of the distressed damsel.

He burst through the door to the outer office to find a most astonishing sight. There, behind the desk of Linda Jones, was the ugliest little monster he had ever seen—green and evil as Ted Turner's socks—wearing his secretary's pink sweater, sitting in her chair and tapping madly at a computer keyboard, a horrible leer spread from ear to demon ear.

"You're not my secretary!" said Daniel Clamp.

The Gremlin responded by grabbing a silex pot of boiling hot water from the nearby coffee station and flinging the water at Clamp.

Daniel Clamp ducked. Clamp played squash, so he had excellent reflexes.

The beastie threw the pot. Clamp ducked again and the pot smashed against a wall.

With a nasty shriek, the punkish Gremlin jumped at Clamp, its claws outstretched, its eyes wild, and commenced ripping and tearing. But Clamp was no 98 pound weakling—not with regular exercise with a trainer in his own personal gym. Clamp batted the thing back successfully, pushing it back like a boxer bashing at an opponnent.

The Gremlin fell back, and its foot fell into the hopper of the huge Ollie North Shredder.

Hating to do it, but seeing no other way of dealing with the thing Daniel Clamp reached over, pushed the ON button. . . .

And he pushed the Mohawked Gremlin down into the shredder.

Chapter
Fifteen

Billy Peltzer raced into the office just in time to witness the demise of Mohawk the Gremlin.

Even for a Gremlin, it was a pretty nasty way to go.

Daniel Clamp was pushing it into the shredder. Mohawk was fighting and squawking all the way, spitting and roaring, but it was no good. Inexorably he was being pushed down through the blades which roared away hungrily, chopping him up real good, sending Gremlin-stuff spattering and splattering in all directions.

Billy winced.

Good riddance though. Billy Peltzer had long since come to the realization that the only good Gremlin was a dismembered or melted Gremlin, a Gremlin rendered incapable of the usual bags of mischief they dispensed.

Yes, Mohawk fought all the way, and only stopped struggling once the last of his odd haircut disappeared within the gnashing blades and gears of the shredder.

Underneath, the glop and shreds shuddered a few times and then were still.

"Sir!" said Billy, rushing up to Daniel Clamp. "Are you all right."

Daniel Clamp seemed to be trying to regain his composure and poise—which was quite difficult for a guy when you're splattered with Gremlin gunk. "I think so—I *hate* using those machines myself."

"Sir, I have to talk to you. There are a—"

Just that moment Frank Forster chose to barge in, fighting to look calm but clearly white as a sheet and quite disheveled. "Mister Clamp, there's a situation in—"

He stopped in his track, staring at the quite yukky remains of Mohawk in the waste bin and still dribbling out from the shredder in nasty gobs.

"My God . . . what. . . . ."

Billy took his opportunity. He had to get his word into the guy really in charge before Forster botched things up totally and thoroughly. "Sir, please listen to me. There are more of these things—maybe lots more. We've got to get people out of the building—and we've got to close the building up. We've got to do it before sundown."

Clamp looked up with alarm and interest. "Yeah? What happens at sundown?"

"These—things can't stand sunlight. It'll kill them. But once it's night time, they can get out, into New York. If that happens—"

Forster pointed an accusing finger at Billy. "He should be in custody. He's dangerous!"

"Dangerous?" Clamp shook his head. "This thing that was in here a minute ago—that was dangerous. This guy's from the art department."

"Yeah?" said Forster his own particular brand of anal-retentive glare directed at Billy Peltzer. "Ask him how he knows so much about these—green things."

"That's a good question, Billy," said Clamp turning to Billy. "How do you know about them?"

"Well, uhm," Billy said. Time to desperately dissemble! "You know that genetics laboratory, down on—"

Clamp's eyes flared. "Of course. Those guys!" He turned to Forster. "I warned you that could be a problem tenant. We could have had three shrinks and a plastic surgeon in that space. But nooooooooo . . ."

"I thought sir . . . I mean I thought that they were part of your whole plan."

"What? Genetics? I do what I understand, Bill, and I certainly don't understand genetics. I've got nothing to do with those people, but clearly I shouldn't have let them into the building. But how do you know so much about them."

"I ... er ... I read science fiction and fantasy!"

"Oh, of course. Yeah, I like sci-fi films—I own the rights to hundreds and hundreds. I've seen 'em all. Horror films too. I especially like that one about the werewolves ... what's it called? THE JOWLING? That one by that nice Italian boy with the nasty sense of humor."

"Sir, we have to get back on track here!" insisted Billy.

"Oh. Right. Sorry Bill."

"Sir," continued Billy. "We have to make sure that none of these things get wet. If that happens ..."

"I'll tell you what we have to do. We have to get a lid on this thing and keep it on. No cops, no media. We'll handle it." He turned to Forster. "Go down to systems control and get on top of this thing."

"Me? Uhm ... but there might be...."

"You're supposed to be getting the bugs out of this building, right? Well, I would call these some pretty major bugs, wouldn't you?"

Forster had to nod with agreement, but he did get a nasty glance at Billy in. "Okay. Right. But I don't think I should try it without an expert." Bitter sarcasm on the last word. "Let's go, pal."

Together Billy and Forster trooped on down to systems control deep in the heart of the Clamp Center.

* * *

Meanwhile, everything in the Clamp Center was going absolutely big-time, old-fashioned, looney tunes crazy.

The Gremlin manifestations were getting worse. Evidently, the Gremlins were multiplying even as they increased in size and danger and total outrageousness.

And Kate, poor dear sweet Kate, was still stuck in that elevator between floors.

Nor did she particularly care for it.

"Help!" she cried. "Help!"

She punched every button on the control panel till her fingers hurt but they were as dead as a grocery store chicken.

The elevator started to rock violently, jerking Kate about willy nilly.

Desperately, Kate punched the alarm button.

Nothing happened.

The only sound she heard was the clamor of countless claws outside, pounding and scraping at the elevator car.

Suddenly, that awful elevator voice started speaking again, resurrected from the dead: "You have selected a floor that is not part of the building at this time..."

Gremlin laughter slid into the elevator like a cascade of cackles straight from the heart of Hell itself. She saw claws tearing from the corners of the elevator, rending through the cheap synthetic material that comprised the elevator car to get in at her.

What could she do?

What she could do, she knew, was not give up. She had fought these little monsters before and won—they were eminently defeatable, just very very persistant and even more numerous.

She shrank away from the sound and the threat, her hands braced against the walls.

Down at the base of the elevator controls was none other than Daffy, the Gremlin.

Chapter Sixteen

In the Splice-o-Life, the cheerful lab technicians worked away on their fun projects, unaware of the chaos that was slowly spreading through the building like fire fusing up toward their big ball of TNT.

Martin and Lewis, the Siamese twins separated only physically, stood over their long table juggling test tubes, vials and petri dishes like circus freaks let loose in a high school science lab.

Their colleague Wally came over to them, carrying a tomato and a handball glove.

Wally said, "Take a look at this, guys. You know how I've been working on making these tomatoes taut for when they ship them?"

Wally slipped on the glove. He flipped the tomato up into the air and then caught it. He slammed it into the wall like a handball, caught it on a bounce and then showed it to the twins.

It wasn't smooshed one little bit!

Lewis said, "That's terrific, Wally....!"

"...top notch!" finished Martin. "How do they taste?"

"That's the best part," said Wally. "We've already had calls from the chefs at two of the airlines."

Suddenly a burp sounded from behind them.

The burp that changed all their lives.

They turned to see that a bunch of Gremlins had overrun one of the lab tables, peering out over the lovely and interesting labscapes— new worlds to conquer!

Now, they had all seen odd things before in their careers—but never quite as odd as these things. They looked like something out of a nightmare.

"Oh my gosh," said Lewis.

"...did somebody leave something out?" said Martin.

"Not me."

Wally said, "Hey! My vegetable medley."

For the naturally inquisitive little demons had moved their scaly and unpleasant selves away from their perches and were exploring the various experimental projects. One had jumped up near the vegetable plants with the tubes.

He grabbed the tube and ate it all.

"No! My experiment!" cried Wally.

The Gremlin grinned evilly. But then his expression changed. He looked like a comic's parody of a drunk who has just taken a shot of very strong liquor.

He did a double take...

...and then the Gremlin started.... *changing.*

The lab boys hadn't seen anything like it since they'd video-taped a tomato plant over a week period on time-exposure. Before their startled eyes, the Gremlin's ears turned into leafy clumps of Romaine Lettuce, bushy and green. The creature seemed to thoroughly enjoy the process, his eyes turning a queasy color of carrot-orange and kale-green.

"No!" cried Wally as the thing, wanting more of this great fun, reached out for another vial of delicious formula.

A claw raked out and Wally jumped back with a torn shirt and scratches down the front of his chest and arm.

"Okay, okay, take it already!"

The Gremlin grinned, chuckled and then grabbed a huge beaker marked CAULI-FLOWER, guzzling it with gusto.

The Gremlin burped, a gust of its breath smelling like V-8 juice after too long in the sun. It started rocking back and forth and suddenly clumps of sickly mutated cauliflower commenced to sprout from its chest, its lips and its nose like a diseased garden.

Nearby, another little monster snagged a beaker marked SEX HORMONE. It downed it quickly, and its face registered immense consumer satisfaction almost immediately.

"My God!"

The guzzling activities of the vile creatures ceased for a moment, their ugly faces swiveling to look over at the new arrival. It was Dr. Catheter, removing his glasses, his hair about a shade whiter and his jaw significantly lowered with astonishment.

With giggles and snarls of amusement, the carnage and guzzling continued apace.

As the Doctor stood in the doorway, one particularly large specimen of Gremlin grabbed a beaker that had been attached to a bulbous brain floating in a nutrient bath. The Gremlin drank down at least a quart of the noxious turquoise stuff.

Martin cried. "Oh no....!"

"....not the brain hormone," finished Lewis.

The spasm hit the gulping Gremlin at about 7.1 on the Richter scale. It began to tremble, its eyes bugging and bobbling, its tongue waggling and gaggling.

It fell over on its back, rolled off the counter and fell head first into a trash can. Its legs twitched.

The can fell over and the Gremlin pushed its way out of it.

Now, perched upon a noble nose was a pair of horn rimmed glasses.

Its lips moved, struggling to emit something...

"I....want....to—"

The Gremlin jumped to his feet, his eyes

suddenly awake and aware, gleaming with intelligence.

It began to speak with a cultured voice rather like George Plimpton in high raconateur mode.

"I want to talk a little bit about what's going on here in this room, because I think there are some fascinating ramifications here for the future." Its arms moved about in high didactic fashion as though lecturing in front of a large audience. "When you introduce genetic material of research quality to a life form such as ours, which is possessed of a sort of—I hesitate to use the word atavism, but let us say a highly *aggressive* nature . . ."

For a moment, the other Gremlins seemed interested with this abrupt change in their fellow. But only a moment. Soon they grew bored and went back to trashing the place, eating and drinking their fill as the scientists tried, in vain, to stop this horrible rampage.

" . . . .for example, that fellow over near there, I believe that's a common bat of the order Chiroptera—the only true mammals, I might add, capable of true flight!"

One of the proliferating gremlins approached the cage of the bat who was Wally's pet project, the one who was being desensitized to light. Connected to the bat's cage by a series of tubing was yet another vial.

Being forever-thirsty, the Gremlin grabbed it and drained it in several quick gulps—Dr. Jekyll-and-Mr. Hyde time again!

The Gremlin stretched out a hand, suprised

and delighted to find a huge expanse of webbing growing between its arm and its side. Both arms. Articulated yet!

The newly intelligent Gremlin cocked its head in a vastly amused fashion and stalked over to its newly changed brother.

"Nice wings! Might I have a brief word with you!"

The Bat Gremlin grinned and looked at Mr. Glasses.

"My friend, you have . . . potential. I want to help you be all that you can be. . . . may I?"

As he continued talking, Mr. Glasses plucked the intravenous tube from the bat's body and happily jammed the needle into the Bat Gremlin's skin.

The bottle with the sunshine logo drained quickly, jacking the Gremlin full of its hormone-and-sunscreen mixture.

The Bat Gremlin's eyes opened wide, wide, wide.

As I'm sure you're aware, sunlight poses a problem for our . . . ethnic group. We don't tan, we don't burn . . . frankly we just become a rather unappetizing sort of photochemical leftover. Thus, this formula . . . specially designed for those of the nocturnal persuasion . . . to make bright light no problem whatever. That will be of crucial usefulness where you'll be going . . ."

Mr. Glasses yanked the IV needle out of the Bat Gremlin's elbow. The Bat Gremlin seemed very enthusiastic at the prospect of unlimited flight in the sunlight—he tilted his head as though asking, "So where do I get to go, Boss?"

"You have wings, my friend," said Mr. Glasses like a pronouncement. "Flap them."

The wings flapped and they flapped with a muscularity and power that within moments pulled it aloft. It floated and flapped about the room, clearly thrilled and excited to be gifted with the power of flight.

The scientists tried to grab it, but to no avail.

"Down! Down!" cried Lewis and Martin.

"To the window, my friend!" cried Mr. Gremlin in a vastly encouraging fashion. "A world of possibilities opens itself to you! Throw off the old constraints...."

The Bat Gremlin hurled itself toward one of the polarized windows, its eyes full of purpose and challenge.

"There it is, the Apple!" cried Mr. Glasses like a British coach, urging his football boys to great heights of acheivement. "The city so nice they named it twice...check it out one time...won't you?"

And the Bat Gremlin slammed into the window, smashing through it and out into the air above the New York streets.

It flapped its wing and it swooped around, a bird released from its cage and crazy with evil joy at its release.

So much havoc to wreak, so much fun to accomplish!

And not only did the bright spring-day sun not bother it, but he actually enjoyed it.

Leaving behind its humble origins, the

newly freed winged off above the streets and buildings of New York City.

Down below, in a park, a pigeon perched upon a lion statue in front of the New York Public Library.

A gob of green goo slammed from above, killing the poor thing instantly.

Chapter
Seventeen

Fred Finlay was taping his show again. He wasn't in a very good mood, either.

For one thing, his beat-up old radio-clock hadn't gone off this morning on time ... And when it had, somehow the tuner had been changed over to a shock rock radio show.

Fred Finlay *hated* rock and roll.

Then the water had gone cold in his shower, he'd cut himself a good one shaving, and the milk had gone off in his refrigerator so that his much-needed cup of coffee had given him absolutely awful heart-burn that not even his usual bottle of Maalox could hurt.

And now this stupid costume was riding up on him and his makeup itched.

So what the hell else could go wrong today?

"Tonight, we've got a classic horror movie

from Grandpa Fred's special dungeon—'' He picked up two film canisters and blew special effects dust off them.

Grandpa Fred was interrupted by a long moan. It wasn't the weak moan from before. No, not by a long shot. It was a genuinely scary, fingernails-on-the-blackboard, creaking crypt-door Inner Sactum style moan.

OHHHHHHHHHHHHHHHHHHHHHH....
MMMMOOOOOOOOOOMMMMMMMMMM-
OOOOOOANNNNNNNNNNNNNNNNN-
NNN..... !

Startled that something should go right this crummy day, Fred Finlay turned around.

Now Fred Finlay had seen some pretty weird things in his day. Even before he'd moved to the House of Freaks that was New York City, he'd traveled the world in the Navy and seen some pretty odd things in obscure Far East, Indian and African ports from Honolulu to Timbucktu.

He was an old coot, Fred was, and he'd pretty much given up on seeing anything that could startle him. But he had to hand it to the things that rose up from behind the gravestones amidst the dry ice ground fog. These guys spooked the hell out of him.

They looked like most of his wife's relatives, God help him, only a little smaller.

He gawked for a moment, then turned back to the control booth and jabbed a thumb back over his shoulder, about to ask the director what the story was with these things.

The director said, "Fred, what's the story with those—things?"

"I . . . I don't. . . ."

One of the Gremlins (for guess what—that's what they were!) grabbed a reel of film from Fred. He pulled it out and held it up against the light. Fake terrified shock washed over the thing's face. It clutched its heart in a fake heart attack and then keeled over onto the floor.

The other creatures laughed uproariously, slapping their knees and knocking each other on the back.

"Uh—that's right," said Grandpa Fred. "It's pretty scary—"

Abruptly, Grandpa Fred was joined by the other two Gremlins. They leaped up on him and put their heads to either side of his, making scary snarls and generally mugging for the camera.

It was clear that they felt in their element here.

"Boy that's creepy," said the director. "Okay, rolling."

Fred finally didn't know quite what to do.

They'd never taught him this might happen to him in TV or drama school.

Oh well. This, after all, was showbiz. And so far this was shaping into the absolute best Grandpa Fred bit yet.

"Uh—" he said, blinking toward the red light at the top of the television camera. "Grandpa Fred and his friends have something *horrible* in store for you tonight!"

The Gremlins bobbed their heads in cheerful agreement.

On the second floor of the arboretum/mall was the token fern and yuppie bar, the Stuffed Olive. Sitting around, sipping beers or, in most cases Perrier and lime or just straight mineral water with a twist.

These, generally, were not Clamp workers. Clamp workers were afraid to be spotted by Forster in the bar. No, these were other workers from other offices in the Center or just tourists.

The Clamp workers went elsewhere for truly serious drinking.

Right now, the few patrons of the bar could have watched a TV set suspended above the central island of metal-spouted liquor bottles. On this TV was a late morning news report. A bland newscaster in a dark suit stared out through the tube.

"There are reports today," he reported, "of major mechanical problems at the Clamp Center office building. Reached by Hotline News, a spokesman for developer Daniel Clamp says there's nothing to worry about, that these are just the normal 'glitches' that a a new building goes through in the first few months. Turning to sports..."

Right next door to the bar was a salad bar. Early lunchers were lined up for their lo-cal roughage.

"My broker says the strongest things in the economy right now are cigarettes and men's magazines," said one patron, a matronly woman.

"Really," said another, trapped but totally without interest.

"Of course, he's been in jail for a while now."

The woman reached down under the salad bar's germ-guard with the plastic tongs to pull a clump of lettuce from the bin.

Instead of a clump of lettuce, she found herself pulling up the vegetable mutant Gremlin.

By now the thing was truly a sight. It had radishes for eyes, corn-row hair, cauliflower ears, stringbean lips and a darting wax-paper tongue.

The other customers recoiled, horrified. The woman tried to pull away but the Vege-Gremlin bared its sharp artichoke teeth, reached out with its carrot fingers and pulled her into vegetable hell through the germ guard.

Back in the Clamp Cable Studios, another show was taping.

The previous year, Clamp had hired a re-spected movie critic to host his own movie review show, THE MOVIE POLICE, part of the growing American trend toward respect for the nuclear family.

Lester Leeds was taping a video show, re-porting on old videos presently getting atten-tion. He had just finished the latest edition of his EVERY MOVIE EVER MADE, PLUS! for

Clamp Publishing, and was just getting deeply into his sex manual, MAKING IT IN THE BALCONY, so it was a relief to get away from his grueling work and under the bright lights of a studio. (Things were getting so bad for poor Lester that he had to ask projectionists to speed up films so that he could get them all in!)

Today, he felt especially happy. He had some real trash to review, and nothing pleased the critic more than to tear apart a film with ripping words and summarily and metaphorically discarding it in the celluloid trash bin.

Lester held up a video-cassette as though he had just picked a particular noisome dead fish up from the garbage.

"And now for our video cassette consumer watch—" It was none other than the much maligned but brilliant watershed effort of cinematic magnificence, second only to CITIZEN KANE in film history, GREMLINS.

Alas, this wretched critic did not care for it.

"Here's one that's just been re-released on video and if you're thinking of renting it, I can think of alot of better things to do with three dollars . . ."

Poor Lester Leeds. Little did he realize it, but three actual genuine real-McCoy Gremlins were sneaking up on him giggling silently and mugging for the camera.

". . . such as burning them. In fact, burning this movie wouldn't be a bad idea. This is a truly, evil, mean-spirited. I don't think there's a single scene more wretched than when poor Mrs. Deagle gets ejected from her automatic chair through her own window into the annals of film history unless it's that bit of monologue about the girl's father caught in the chimney at Christmas time! Awful! Don't these people know that Christmas is a sacred holiday. Boy, these guys are truly mentally disturbed. In fact—"

The Gremlins leaped upon the nasty (and quite wrong) critic, dragging him off the couch. Leeds turned around in mid-plunge to see the creatures intent on mauling, and he figured maybe he'd opened his mouth once too often.

"Wait! No! I was kidding! Look—" He pushed up his thumbs. "Two thumbs up ... Two thumbs. ... Argggggghhhhhh!"

And in Hollywood, producers roared their approval.

Chapter
Eighteen

Down in the Clamp Center's mall, a small stock brokerage, Bux, Junkke and Jaille operated out of a very small set of cubicles they hesitated to call an office. Indeed, it was known merely as a euphemistic "business station" even to its owners.

At his desk, Harry Mishkin, a broker from Teaneck, New Jersey, was trying to unload some questionable utility stocks on a real rube from Long Island.

Suddenly, however, he found himself confronted by a demonish-looking creature who rather reminded him of the way his head felt after the Black Monday crash of '87.

He opened his mouth to say hello, but only "Arrgggggh!" came out.

"What's wrong!" said a voice of the frightened client over the phone. "Oh my God! The market's crashed again. Oh my god, and all my money's in junk bonds!"

"No . . . No . . . No crash here. . . . Oh Jeez. No problem, think about those stocks. . . . oh jeez. 'Bye!"

He hung up.

Harry Mishkin had looked at some nasty clients over his martinis at his power lunches, but this guy took the cake.

The thing stuck up an accusing claw toward Mishkin's fire engine red tie.

Mishkin started yanking it off. If this thing wanted his tie, it could have it. But the thing seemed not so intent on things as in creating general mayhem. The Gremlin swiped at him and Mishkin dodged.

Other Gremlins swarmed in, kicking the brokers out of their offices, grabbing their phones and screaming, "Buy! Sell! Buy! Sell!"

Mishkin tried to run, but he tripped and fell into the supervisors office. The supervisor had long since vacated his office, and there was one of the monsters from Wall Street Hell, this one with glasses and a phone in one hand.

"Oh, yes," the Gremlin was saying into the phone. "I'd say it's a full-scale panic. Are you having a run on the bank there yet? Well, it's rather brutal here . . . we're advising our clients to put everything they've got into canned food and shotguns. . . . yes . . ."

Mishkin managed to put himself back on his feet and get the hell out of there, wishing he were high up enough to jump out a window.

These things were going to send the stocks and bonds market into a tailspin!

Thank God he didn't invest in the things.

Kate Berringer, bruised, haggard and splattered with Gremlin blood managed to make it upstairs to a stairwell door.

She opened it.

Complete mayhem reigned in the lobby.

As panicking customers and office workers tried to flee the swarming Gremlins, Kate saw that the things were simply all over the place.

Gremlins were on the frozen yogurt stand, shooting streams of whipped cream at fleeing workers. A bartender fell to the floor, trying to shake the things off. The vegetable Gremlin was absolutely destroying the salad bar.

A woman screamed and ducked as a gremlin swung toward her on a sparking electric cable torn from the ceiling. People in general were desperately scrambling toward the exit doors, but tripping up like crazy, for the place had been trashed into a veritable obstacle course.

Kate took momentary cover behind a pillar, gathering her nerve—then she made a break across the lobby, running for a fire alarm on the back wall.

Abruptly, a Gremlin jumped out in front of her.

She was quite prepared to do battle using what little she knew from the kung fu course she'd taken at the Y—but the Gremlin didn't seem interested in fighting.

He wore a gray raincoat and as soon as he stepped out in front of her, he flung it open, flashing her.

Kate, disgusted, used a kung fu kick to clear the way and then jumped for the red alarm. She pulled it, expecting a loud clanging, or at the very least some sort of ringing.

But no.

Not in the Clamp Center!

Instead, melodramatic music built under a voice that sounded like the guy on PBS's NATURE show:

"Giver of warmth, destroyer of forests, right now, this building is on fire."

Upstairs, an office worker, unaware of the chaos below, was traveling along. He stopped to listen, totally baffled.

"What?"

"Yes, the building is on fire. Leave the building. Enact the age old drama of self-preservation."

"Fire!" cried another worker. "Fire."

General panic swept through the entire skyscraper.

Elsewhere in New York City, the Futtermans were enacting the age-old ritual of tourism.

Since Sheila Futterman was a real fan of gothic architecture, she had really wanted to see the famous Cathedral of Saint Eva Marie on Fifth Avenue.

Murray Futterman wasn't so thrilled. Murray didn't particularly care to go out into the open much. After the war, Murray never did particularly have good nerves, and after that awful business back in Kingston Falls with the (cringe) Gremlins driving that snow plow through his place and into him (a lot of people thought he was dead, but he'd just had a severe case of shock) he mostly just wanted to stay inside and futz with his stamp collection and model airplanes. But he'd been in therapy now for years, and with the love and patience of his dear wife Sheila, he was coming out of it enough so that he could make this trip. Seeing the boys from the old 85th Squadron was important to Murray, damned important, but he sure needed Sheila's support in braving this hurly-burly, topsy-turvy, close-up in-your-face city.

So if Sheila Futterman wanted to go and see the Statue of Liberty or the Radio City Music Hall or the Cathredral of Saint Eva Marie or freakin' Grant's Tomb for that matter, then by God, Murray Futterman was going to go with her.

He didn't have to like it, and he would go around with a sour face and make disparaging remarks, but Sheila deserved the best, the very freakin' best.

They were standing on the other side of the street now from the Cathredral so that Sheila could click off a couple of pictures on her Nikon. Murray, he was much more interested in the shoddy construction work these New

York hard-hat bozos were doing on the sidewalk. Cripes, the stuff they were pouring was
clearly more sand than cement and they
seemed far more interested in the women's
short skirts passing by than in mixing the stuff
in their mixer or leveling it down right.
Sheesh, it made Murray crazy just watching
this gross misuse of taxpayer's bucks!

Sheila was far too involved in her appreciation of the building before them to pay
much attention to this mess beside them.

"Oh, Murray! What a beautiful building!"
she enthused.

Murray Futterman looked back up to the
huge and towering catheral. It was of dark
granite, stark in contrast with the dunnish
gray remainder of normal New York. It was
an old style medieval cathedral, complete
with flying butrresses and gargoyles, to say
nothing of long stretches of stained glass. Of
course, in this hellhole of a city, you had to
put up bars and wire to protect the glass, so
you rather had the effect of a building of God
under siege.

"Beautiful?" said Murray. "Looks like
something outta the freakin' dark ages!"

"Well, of course, dear. That's the idea."

"Huh? What's somethin' like that doin' in
the middle of a city, for God's sake? It belongs
back over the ocean. Boy did I see a slew of
these things bombed out, back in the Big
War!"

"That's nice, Murray. But it's getting close
to the time that we can take the tour. I've been

so looking forward to a tour of the Cathredral of Saint Eva Marie, Murray."

"Yeah," said Murry Futterman mordantly. "Maybe we'll get a handout from the poor box. We need it, after what I'm paying in this city."

"Murray, look at those lovely gargoyles."

Murray had already looked at the gargoyles, thank you, and he didn't like what he saw.

Mostly because they reminded him of the G-word things that had almost killed him.

He didn't comment on this, he just grunted and turned back at the much more remarkable sight of shoddy hard hat workers slumming on their job.

"Murray. Oh my God, Murray! What's that?"

Murray turned around and looked, expecting maybe to see a mugging in progress. Anyway Murray Futterman didn't expect to be surprised by *anything* he saw in this crazy city.

Murray Futterman was more than surprised, though. He was shocked.

One of those stone birds ... gargoyles Sheila called them. The bastard was freakin' *moving*!

It had been sitting up there, perched on a corner like its cronies, all still and stony, and now it was flapping its wings, alive.

Murray opened his mouth and all that came out was "Hey!"

"What is it Murray?" said Sheila.

Oh my God! That awful and familiar face, with the ears like Satan's was tilting down, scouring the crowd fiercely!

And it was looking straight at Murray Futterman!

"No!" he said.

The thing left its perch, flapping its bat wings. It dove down toward the crowd, talons outstretched, hellish eyes flaring.

"It's them!" cried Murray Futterman. "It's *them!*" He turned around, hands held out imploringly to the New Yorkers passing by. "Help me! Somebody help me!"

It was his absolute worse nightmare come true! Everything he thought he had control of in his life suddenly felt thoroughly shattered.

And the New Yorkers totally ignored him, trudging forward in their typical hides-of-leather New York manner, oblivious.

He turned, feeling about ready to have a nervous breakdown.

But he didn't have time to. The winged Gremlin was upon him.

"Sheila!" He cried. "Get away, Sheila."

The winged Gremlin slashed at his jacket, ripping it. Futterman pushed his wife away to safety, steeled himself and then gave the Gremlin a hard right to the kisser.

"Okay, you bastard! You asked for it, you got it."

The blow barely fazed the Gremlin.

It was on Futterman like a cheap suit, fluttering and clawing, pushing him back toward the crowd. It was a scene straight out of one of the Ray Harryhausen Sinbad movies.

Futterman grappled with the thing. He grabbed it by the neck and flung it into the churning cement mixer. The creature squealed. The mixer tilted, dumping the Gremlin and its load into the larger mass of liquid concrete.

The thing struggled in this glop awhile like the Swamp Thing in his element. Some of the wet cement dropped off, but nonetheless as the bat Gremlin flapped aloft, there remained a veneer of wet cement on its body and wings.

It forgot its mad and senseless attack on Futterman, lurching instead back toward its previous perch on the cathedral.

There it settled, stiffening, stiffening. . . .

. . . until it became a genuine, unmoving gargoyle.

Futterman stared at this sight with astonishment—but mostly with a sense of profound accomplishment. He felt as though a gigantic burden had been lifted from his shoulders.

He'd done it.

He'd stood up to one of the things, and he'd beaten it. After years of feeling weak and useless, quite suddenly he felt powerful again.

In charge.

He turned and found his faithful wife Sheila, by his side as always.

He grabbed her arm and pulled her along toward the east side of town.

"Murray—where are you going?" she demanded, clearly not at all recovered from the shocking incident that had just occurred to them.

"To the Clamp Center," he said. "We have

to tell Billy. The Gremlins are loose again!
Come on!"

It wasn't far.

Together they started running.

Chapter
Nineteen

Between the floors of the Clamp Center, the insanity escalated and elevated.

It even climbed up and down the steps on its own.

The fire alarm had sent people into a panic and they were spilling down the halls in great raging numbers. Of course since there was no smoke they didn't have much real cause to fear fire. But those of the more privileged actually saw clumps of the rampaging Gremlins—and news of the monster infestation spread even faster than wildfire.

Billy Peltzer didn't have the luxury of panic.

He knew he had to stay together, stay *rational* and in control. He knew better than anyone how to deal with these things, and

since it was his fault they were loose again—
well, it was his responsibility to stop them.

Just exactly *how*, Billy hadn't the faintest
idea—but he was going to have to do it some
way.

Billy and Forster were hurrying down the
hall, headed for the Systems Control Center.
It was there, Billy hoped, that they could get
a grip on the problem.

As they hurried, though, they suddenly en-
countered a stream of lab animals, scrambling
down the hall like escapees from Noah's ark.
Mice, monkeys, rats, rabbits scampered and
scurried under their legs.

Following them was none other than an
older man in a lab coat, eyes crazed, his grey
hair mussed and his glasses askew. Billy recognized him as Dr. Catheter, the head researcher from Splice-of-Life.

"The horror! The horror!" Dr. Catheter
cried. "The *breakage!*

Billy stopped him. "Doctor.... What? What
happened?"

"Yeah, pal," said Forster. "What the hell's
going on? Did you crazies cause all this carnage?"

Catheter seemed to totally ignore Forster's
question.

"I swear to God...I will never...hurt anything again...they are all part of the great
chain of being....there are things that man
was not meant to splice..."

"What the hell is he talking about?" demanded Forster.

"Try and calm down—" said Billy. "Where were the—

There. The novelizer, Mr. David Bischoff, Esq., has been successfully waylaid and is now tied up in the bathroom of his Los Angeles apartment.

Do not attempt to adjust your book.

We have control of the programming.

Please excuse the rudeness. You have previously known me as the "Gremlin that drank the brain fluid"—or, as Bischoff quaintly called me, Mr. Glasses. Believe it or not, in the screenplay, I am referred to as BRAIN GREMLIN.

I want to take this opportunity to talk to you about our philosophy toward life, so that we will not be misunderstood and branded as "monsters."

Yes, but faithful novel readers, I do not intend to cheat you. In the movie presentation, Gremlins take over the movie theatre (ah, what a delicious conceit—excellent, Joe— was that you?) and Hulk Hogan comes to the rescue.

I do believe that Kenneth Tobey of THE THING is somewhere in there.

However, let us now deal with more intellectual matters.

In the great paradigm of anti-intellectualism that is the vast American untermenchen, there needs be a seismic quake of thought, a veritable avalanche of anarchy, to goose you somnambulent beings from your couch-potato torpor.

May I offer you the services of we Gremlins. You may hereafter refer to us as the New Capitalist Democratic Nice Folks.

Already our numbers are spreading out from the heart of America to aid you in this endeavor and although you may be viewing this physically for the first time now (except for those lucky citizens of Kingston Falls who received a foreshadow some years ago) our intellectual forces have been at work for some time, albeit embodied in human form.

According to my contacts with our crypto-CD's the Church of the SubGenius it is generally not known, for instance, that the entirety of network television is programmed by proto-Capalist Democrats.

However, the past is merely prologue, introduction, forward, with some long footnotes thrown in.

Our time is now!

So, my dear readers (oh, the few, the chosen literate who have been intelligent enough to purchase this volume) prepare for a New Age of the New Capitalist Demo—

Oh, dear. Mr. Bischoff seems to have successfully axed his way out of the bathroom.

Methinks I need to fly and return this temporarily liberated keyboard to his superb, urbane and witty prose—

Back I fly to the Clamp Cent. . . . .

Chapter
Twenty

Gremlins amok in a genetic lab! Boy, high concept time in Hollywood. Sounds like big b.o. And good box office too!

Billy Peltzer wasn't thinking much about Hollywood films as he ran to the Splice of Life labs. He was trying to figure out how to contain this havoc on the half-shell.

When he arrived, the Gremlins were chomping and guzzling away, going through all kinds of contortions, flopping about willy-nilly, shuddering and generally ripping through a series of changes like something in a Joe Dante film from Hell.

Billy spotted a Gremlin at a lab table, grabbing for a vial containing a crackling, zapping fluid. The vial was labeled with a stylized lightning bolt.

The Gremlin did not merely drink the stuff, he swallowed the entire vial with a profound "Ga-LUNK!" sound.

Billy stood back, expecting some kind of change. But nothing happened. There was no transformation.

However, the Gremlin seemed inordinately attracted to a wall socket. It stepped forward and put its claw out toward the plug hole. As soon as the claw touched, there was a loud clap of thunder, and the entire Gremlin exploded into a neon catastrophe of power. It's light-outlined body shuddered for a moment, and then the Gremlin—changed into a being of raw current—was sucked into the plug.

Oh great, thought Billy. Wonderful! The electric company was going to be absolutely thrilled.

In another part of the room, Frank Forster was having heavy dating problems. His new amour, a beautifully made-up Gremlin with purple hair, a tight, short, sequined dress and awful lips, was hanging onto his leg while he tried to escape through the door.

"Look, lady," he was saying. "You don't want me! You really don't want me! All my girlfriends dump me! So why don't you!"

However the girl Gremlin seemed absolutely smitten and intent upon her goal.

Gremlin seduction!

Meanwhile, Dr. Catheter, like his idol Dr. Moreau, was having a bit of difficulty with the tranformed beasties. He stuck his hand in the cabinet, expecting to pull out a 12 gauge or one of his Uzis. Instead, he pulled out a Gremlin, its teeth buried into his arm. Trying to shake it off, the scientist went tripping through the wrecked lab, crashing into the equipment. A number of other Gremlins, seeing the guy and doubtlessly sensing a mad scientist, jumped upon him and sent him stumbling to the floor.

Billy had other things to worry about, though. He had spotted one of the Mohawked Gremlins at a particularly dangerous spot, fooling with a cage containing the biggest tarantula that Billy could imagine. Upon the cage hung a bottle, connected to the hairy body of the tarantula by a surgical tube.

Right, thought Billy. Essence of huge spider. There was absolutely no question about what kind of beastie this Gremlin would turn into.

Not only that, it would be a huge beastie.

He had to stop this unholy communion, so he hurried over to the scene, grabbing up a length of piping to club the thing with.

However, his intervention was not to be . . .

For just as he reached the mohawked Gremlin, lightning arced across the room from AC outlet to AC outlet, forming a horror-comics configuration of a Gremlin, sketched in jagged electricity. The thing zapped across the gap, getting in between Billy and the Gremlin at the spider table, forcing him to back away.

Giggling, the Mohawked Gremlin grabbed the vial and hurried away, escaping the lab.

Cackling and crackling, the electric Gremlin arced across the air spraying the area with a profound smell of ozone. Billy was thrown back, his hair standing on end.

Fortunately, the thing swam toward a table chock full of scientific gadgetry. Included amongst this collection was a large cyclotron.

The Electro-Gremlin touched it and it started spinning crazily. It bent over to examine it closer and was sucked by electromagnetic forces directly into the motor, shorting out in a showering explosion of sparks and smoke.

Billy heaved a sigh of relief.

Fortunately, the Electro-Gremlin would be contained in there.

But he knew this reprieve from melodrama would not last long.

And if that Gremlin got into the New York City power plants, God alone knew the havoc it would cause.

Daniel Clamp sat in his office, trying not to be overwhelmed by all this craziness.

And he thought that his buddy Donald Trump had had problems with that Ivana thing! Boy! This was much *much* worse! Dealing with a skyscraper full of little green monsters was as bad as . . .

As. . . .

Well, it was almost as bad as a skyscraper full of *lawyers* for God's sake!

He had a fifth of his favorite Oh-Crap-What-A-Hell-of-A-Day whiskey, in one hand and his telephone in the other and he'd just taken a swallow out of one and was talking into the other to his PR firm:

"Yeah, right. For God's sake, the people are going to survive, the building's going to survive . . . But I need some public relations damage control here. . . . what do you tell them? Tell them everything's under control, we've just had a few problems and we're getting everything under control and—"

Something attracted his attention. One of the monitors, previously blank, showed a card scrawled with the words CLAMP CABLE NEWS NETWORK. The sign dropped away, to reveal a badly composed and shaky minicam image of the lobby. Little green monsters—the things that Bill Peltzer had called "Gremlins"—were creating total carnage. But this was not what fully drew Clamp's utter astonishment.

"A live report from the center of the Clamp Building. Crisis! We have been invaded! This invasion by strange creatures, perhaps from another galaxy . . . or a *dimensional warp!*"

"Dracula . . ." said Clamp.

There was a guy in a Dracula costume, holding a CCNN mike, doing a live reporting spot. It was Grandpa Fred—from the "Late Creature Feature!"

The camera, wobbling, caught a fast glimpse of Gremlins in kids' clothes frolicking past in the background.

". . . and, just a moment ago," said Grandpa Fred, his eyes growing wide as saucers, putting a bit of horrorshow spin on his delivery, "in a *spinetingling*, *bloodchilling* incident..." He seemed to catch himself, and turned back to a staccato David Brinkley delivery. "Uh—they continue to plague this troubled structure throughout what has been a turbulent and tumultuous afternoon..."

"Oh, shit," said Clamp.

Not only was this a goddamned news leak!

It was being leaked by one of the Undead in velvet drag....

Who looked like Grandpa Munster yet!

"Herb!" said Clamp. "Do you have a division that deals with bad P.R. *hemorhaging?*"

Outside the Clamp Building, at the edge of the crowd, one of the less fortunate TV newspeople, unable to get inside for the juicy bits, was arguing with a cop.

"Look, just let us in there," he was saying. "We'll take the responsibility—"

"Forget it, pal," said the sterling example of New York's finest, his lunch of beer and donuts still on his breath. "Most of the people are out of there now, anyway."

"Then who's in there? Look, I've been in Beirut—"

"Oh yeah? I bet they miss you there." He pushed the guy back, looking as though he'd like to take the mike and jam it down his throat. Then the cop addressed the crowd. "Let's move back, folks."

Just then the wailing that had been just in the background solidified into two bright red fire engines pulling up, parting the crowd.

Firemen piled out and connected their hoses to hydrants and cops pushed the crowd back to clear a path to the door for the firemen.

It was at that moment that the Futtermans arrived.

Murray Futterman was breathing hard, and so was Sheila, but by golly they'd made it all those blocks to the Clamp Building and by gosh Murray was going to *do* something.

He wasn't gonna let those goddamned little monsters *push him around anymore!*

Murray spotted a TV newsguy interviewing a flowsy looking disheveled lady—

"Murray! That's Microwave Marge! I watch her all the time! She's the one who taught me how to make the microwave corn-doodle chowder!"

Murray elbowed his way forward toward the newsguy ... He had to speak his mind, goddamnit!

"And ... and then," Microwave Marge was saying. "And then these *horrible green things* came into the kitchen and they, they put all kinds of metal utensils and cooking ware into the units, the ovens which you should never never do—it's not like your conventional oven, it produces a ... a reaction and it ex-ploded, and the horrible things were, they were *laughing, and—*"

Cripes! thought Futterman. Those creatures were already at it! They were probably swarming all over the inside of the building!

"They must practically be spilling outta

the office by now," he fretted to the Missus, who could only goggle at the excitement, trying to get her breath back from the run. She was pointing animatedly over to where the fire engines had pulled up to the curb. Raincoated and helmeted firemen had just affixed hoses to plugs and were about ready to turn on the water pressure.

"Yikes!" said Murray Futterman. Big no no! Geez, if those sprays of water hit those Gremlins!

"Hold it!" screamed Futterman, running over and blocking the entrance so that the firemen couldn't get past. He was waving his arms like a madman. "Wait! No water!"

"What!' said the foremost fireman, baffled.

"It's not fire in there—I don't care if the alarm *is* on. It's *Gremlins*. If you get water on 'em, they just *multiply!*" He turned to the cop nearby. "You gotta let me in there! I know how to deal with the problem!"

Sheila suddenly found her voice. "Murray!"

But Murray Futterman knew what he had to do. Nope, he wasn't afraid of no Gremlins now—but what scared the shit out of Murray Futterman right now was the idea of those things getting out of hand, reproducing and spilling out into the rest of the world!

But the cop blocked the would-be savior's path.

"Uh, sure, pal—look, why don't you calm down a little? Just—"

"Don't talk to me like I'm crazy—" And

then it hit him like a ton of bricks. The whole magilla. The great big ball of wax. "I was *never* crazy. I'm *fine!*"

Sheila grabbed him and held him close. "Of course you are, Murray! I told you that all along!"

"I'm fine!" He turned back to address the people in the crowd. "There really *are* Gremlins, and they're in the Clamp Center right now . . . little big eared monsters who are just the evilest little imps you ever saw! *And I'm not crazy!*"

The folks in the crowd, of course, did not seem to agree with that estimation.

Billy Peltzer raced into Daniel Clamp's office.

He needed help, and Daniel Clamp was the only one that could give it to him.

Clamp was pacing his office fretfully. When he saw Billy coming toward him, he looked up with hope in his face.

"Billy—how's it going out there? Any progress? Just tell me there's progress!"

"I'm afraid it's pretty bad right now, sir—"

"Bad? It's horrible," said Clamp. "There are *people* in this building. Real lives. You have any idea what kind of *lawsuits* we're looking at here?"

"Yes sir. We'll have to—"

But just as he was speaking, he heard a sick-making, familiar crackling sound. He turned around in time to see the Electro-Gremlin doing its strange arcing dance just short of the ceiling—coming this way!

Clamp saw it too.

"Help!" he cried.

Hardly even thinking about what he was doing, Billy grabbed the receiver of a videophone, and stepped between Clamp and the Electro-Gremlin. As though the receiver was a catcher's mitt, he put it up between Clamp and the Electro-Gremlin.

The thing zapped into the receiver and with an electrical conflagration, it disappeared inside.

"Good grief, look at that!" said Clamp.

The Electro-Gremlin was caught inside the videophone's screen. Trapped, it was writing in electro-rage as recorded voice bounced around it and issued from the phone's speaker.

Recorded voices rattled from the speakers:

"If you want to make a call, please hang up and try again . . .

"We're sorry—all circuits are busy now. . . ."

Billy looked up to Clamp. "He's in the phone system on hold. That should take care of him for a while."

Another recorded voice announced, "While waiting, we invite you to listen to a brief interlude of recorded music."

The Music started playing. It was a cheery Mantovani meets the Muzak version of "Raindrops Keep Falling on my Head" segueing into a spritely "Memories" from CATS.

The Electro-Gremlin writhed, its rage turned into total agony.

Daniel Clamp looked up, his honest and open American face filled with honest and open appreciation, recognition. "Uh, Bill—thanks."

"Sure. Mister Clamp, we have to stop these things from leaving the building. If they get out, that's it for New York—*at least* New York."

Another look on that open and honest Jimmy Stewart face. Consternation. A grave nod, and then Daniel Clamp, looking like a Midwestern mortician of a previous century just requested to inter Abraham Lincoln, opened a drawer and removed a videocassette. "I thought this would never run, Bill—but maybe it will."

"What is it?"

"The sign-off. The big sign-off."

He put the tape into a VCR under his wall monitors. Several monitors filled with a montage of images. Beautiful shots of animals, sunsets, beaches, tranquil streams. Profound and deep New Age electronic music streamed from stereo speakers as a narrator intoned resonant words:

"Because of the end of civilization, the Clamp Cable Network now leaves the air. We hope you have enjoyed our programming—but, more important, we hope you have enjoyed.....life."

A bright teenage girl-singer's voice poured over the continuing montage like treacle, singing a sprightly version of an old hymn. "Yet in my dreams I be, Nearer my God to thee..."

Clamp turned away from the images, his chest swelling with emotion. He wiped away a tear with his forefinger. "It's beautiful, isn't it?"

"Yes," said Billy. He was looking at the complex tapestry of controls. "Listen, sir, can you set the clocks in the building ahead three hours? All of them?"

Clamp looked like a schoolmarm about to discipline a student. "Bill, there's nothing we can't do in this building. Why?"

"Sunlight kills these things. That's why they're still in here. But when it's sundown— or when they think it is—they'll all get together in one place so they can go out. They'll all be in the the lobby."

"Right," said Clamp. That's the only way out. The front doors." He whipped a pocket Wizard from his jacket and tapped orders into a mini-keyboard, then examined the results. "The sun sets at—seven-twenty-five."

"So around four-twenty—just before they try to leave—that's when we can make our move."

"I like that. They're off balance, we've got information they don't. That's when you can really take someone out." He blinked, then looked again at Billy. "By the way, Bill. What is our move?"

"It's just an idea...you'll have to set it up. From outside the building, if you can get out there."

"Yeah—I've got my own entrance. You should get out too."

"There's some things I still have to take care of in here. Things . . . and people."

"This idea of yours—"

"Yeah. Is going to be tricky. But if it works—you could save the city."

"Save the city." Clamp smoothed his finger across imaginary headlines in the sky. " 'DEVELOPER SAVES CITY!' Good. Shoot."

Billy Peltzer got moving.

Chapter
Twenty-one

Of all the outrage that his Gremlin progeny had put him through, this was the worst.

Gizmo struggled against his bonds, once again wishing that he had not been so curious, once again cursing himself (although this was very difficult for Mogwais since the creatures had no cursewords in their vocabulary—the closest was "stinky ice cream" and "not-good person") for crawling out of that drawer, directly into water and much, much trouble.

George and Lenny and a raft of Mohawked Gremlins had been putting him through Hell (or, in Mogwai language, unHeaven). He didn't know how he'd survived the incredibly perverse Choo-choo train torture, and the absolutely ungodly game of raquetball with Gizmo as the ball.

But survived he had, which had given George an even *nastier idea*, an idea which they were implementing now with great Gremlin glee, an idea straight out of Edgar Allen Gremlin.

They were in the copy shop. Gizmo was tied with heavy twine to the top of a paper-cutting table. Above him, George hung by one arm from a high shelf. In his other claw, George held a pendulum rigged from a T-square, a protractor, rubber bands. At the end, gleaming in the candle light and occasionally blurred by the incense they were burning, was a razor sharp blade knife. George swung the pendulum. The knife blade moved closer to Gizmo's chest. Closer, closer, closer, each pass.

The Mohawked Gremlin cackled at Gizmo's dilemma. He paced back and forth beside the torture scene. Like a melodramatic villain swilling whiskey, he slurped the liquid from the vial he'd stolen in the genetics lab. On the label was a picture of a spider...

As the blade moved closer, grazing Gizmo's fur, the Mogwai finally realized that if he didn't do something, it would be very bad for him.

The blade sliced the top of the twine, loosening its grip on him.

Gizmo's attitude toward these things had always been denial and fear. He'd always shoved them to the back of his mind when they weren't around, and tried to get away from them when they were. But now, the beasties had gone too far. Gone too far, even for a peaceloving, gentle kind Mogwai like Gizmo.

Yep. They'd pushed *this* Mogwai *too far*.

For a moment, Gizmo saw black. He pushed at his restraints with a strength that he did not know he had.

The bonds burst, the blackness fled and Gizmo knew *exactly* what he had to do. *Exactly*.

George grabbed the T-square like a scythe and tried to hack at Gizmo with the knife blade.

But Gizmo grabbed the pendulum and pulled down so hard that George tumbled from the shelf. The torturer landed on the Mohawked Gremlin. While the Gremlins were in a heap, Gizmo scrambled away toward the door. Lithely leaping an outstretched claw, he headed down the corridor.

Billy! He had to find Billy!

Together, maybe they could stop this madness!

And then they could have some dinner. Gizmo was starving!

Marla Bloodstone stepped into the corridor, looking for somebody anybody. The hallway was dim and deserted, and Marla got this creepy-crawly feeling that she didn't like at all.

"Isn't anybody *working* around here?" she cried out, putting out a brave front of indignation. "Come on...I need some *light* in my—"

Abruptly a booming voice from the multitude of hidden speakers stopped her in her tracks. "—not stealing office supplies works for me, and the way I live today..."

"What!"

The voice, a female's, continued: "When I save money for the Clamp organization, I feel good about myself *all over!"*

The voice sped up to an unintelligible squeak.

"What the hell is going on!"

She moved off into a foyer area, and then into an even darker passage. Blast it all! A girl needed some *light* to get around!

She stumbled forward....

And she suddenly ran into something, something that gave slightly, but was sticky. She couldn't get off it.

Desperately, in the dim light, she looked about to see what it was and her heart nearly stopped.

Ohmigod. It was a big-hairy-spider web.

She was so panicked that she couldn't even scream.

Cockroaches Marla had learned to live with. You live in New York City, you learn to live with rats and cockroaches and foreign cab drivers.

But spiders...

Marla Bloodstone *hated* spiders.

"Help me!" she cried. "Somebody please help me!"

But her voice echoed away, unanswered.

Wall-Street-crash stocking-run backed-up-toilet *panic!*

She was never going to make her deadline now!

Outside the Clamp building, the sky was heading toward dark. The firemen still had their hoses connected to the hydrants and were just waiting for the first hint of smoke to start gushing, despite Murray Futterman's desperate pleas to get the water away from the Gremlins.

Nonetheless, he was getting pushed back by the cops while he screamed at the firemen till he was blue in the face. "Listen to me! No water! I'm telling you, don't squirt the little bastards or they're going to take over the world!"

A commotion rippled through the crowd.

Something was happening on the side of the building.

From a sidewalk elevator in front of a delicatessen, Daniel Clamp stepped out toward the crowd. Immediately he was mobbed by reporters.

"Mister Clamp, is it true that the building's been evacuated?" asked one, waving a mike forward, desperate for a comment.

"Sir, is the building on fire?"

"No, no," said Clamp. He gestured the firemen away. "That's a false alarm. We've just got some problems—"

"Problems?" said another newscaster.

"You've got a guy in a Dracula costume in there, broadcasting stuff with little green monsters. Are you trying to panic New York City?"

"Absolutely not," said Clamp.

"Then the monsters are *real?*"

"I didn't say that," Clamp snapped. He was a master of this news conference business and he could deal with these guys easily.

He moved off, taking the mob with him.

Murray Futterman wasn't watching though. Murray Futterman was looking at that open elevator. That was the way in, thought Futterman. That was the way to get to the Gremlins.

He ran for the doors, hit the button.

The doors closed up.

"Murray!" cried Sheila Futterman.

But it was too late. Murray was inside the elevator and heading down under the street before anyone could do anything.

Murray Futterman was inside!

Murray Futterman smiled to himself and took a deep breath. Okay you bastards! Get ready! 'Cause Murray Futterman is comin' to kick your little scrawny *butts!*

Boy what a scoop!

Fred Finlay, a.k.a. Grandpa Fred, was absolutely charged with excitement. He'd not only lucked into a chance to cover the news here as a reporter, going from scene of crises to scene of carnage, but now he could actually make like one of his idols, Mike Wallace. He could actually interview one of them.

Fred, still in his Count Dracula outfit, sat upon a plush couch. The Japanese cameraman (who'd actually done an absolutely splendid job on this whole thing) crouched before him, pulling back on his shot to get in Grandpa Fred and the ... uhm ... person he was interviewing, there on the other side of the couch, looking as comfortable and in control as Gore Vidal promoting one of his snide and misanthropic American historical epics.

"And in an even more bizarre twist," he said to the camera, effecting a just-the-facts-ma'am Mike Wallace pose, "one of the creatures—" He turned to his "guest." "'Creatures'—is that accurate?"

The Gremlin nodded.

It was Mr. Glasses, looking calm and reposed, smoking a cigarette in a holder, wearing a suit and a cravate and, of course, his horn-rimmed glasses.

Katsuji grinned and bobbed his head excitedly, working the controls of his camera.

"One of the creatures," said Fred to the Camera, "who is able to talk and he's going to talk to us now." Back to the smart Mr. Glasses. "I think the main question people have is—well, what do you want."

Mr. Glasses turned to the camera, his cultured tones undulating into the microphone. "Fred, what we want is, I think, what everyone wants and what your viewers have." A significant raise of eyebrows. "... civilization."

From somewhere (doubtless the bar) came the cheers of the Gremlins as they clapped and pounded mugs and pitchers of beer on table tops.

"The niceties, Fred," continued Mr. Glasses. "The fine points. Diplomacy. Compassion. Standards, manners, tradition. That's what we're reaching toward. Oh, we may stumble along the way, but—civilization, yes. The Geneva Convention. Chamber music. Susan Sontag. Everything your society has worked so hard to accomplish over the centuries—that's what we aspire to. We want to be civilized. I mean, you take a look at this fello here—" As it happened a dopey looking Gremlin was wandering onto the set, grinning stupidly.

Mr. Glasses pulled a gun out of his coat, aimed and shot him dead.

From the bar came the sound of Gremlin cheering.

"Now, was that civilized? No. I think not. Fun yes. Civilized, in absolutely no sense."

Grandpa Fred, at first merely shocked, decided that sitting here on this couch with this clearly quite mad talking monster with a smoking gun was not a good idea. "Well, uh, of course that could be argued in different ways..."

"We want the essentials, Fred," said Mr. Glasses, waving the smoking gun around carelessly. "Dinettes. Bar stools. Complete bedroom groups. Convenient credit, even if we've been turned down in the past. Fred, am I losing you here...?"

You bet he was losing him.

Gesturing at Katsuji desperately to abandon ship, Grandpa Fred was getting the hell out of there!

Outside, Billy's plan was being implemented by Clamp.

The sun still had an hour to go, but inside the electronic (and centrally controlled) clocks had been pushed ahead a full three hours...

As the crowd watched, workers with cranes positioned a cloth theatrical backdrop—a scene from the Red Square in Moscow—in front of the doors.

"A little to the left," said Clamp, supervising. "Careful, careful...."

A fire chief climbed down from a newly arrived hook and ladder truck. He pulled his metal cap back and scratched his head. "What's this thing for?"

Clamp pointed toward the building. "These monster things can only come out when it's dark. We've put all the clocks in the building ahead three hours. When they think it's sunset...and they see what a nice 'night' it is outside...they'll be in the lobby, getting ready to come out. When they do, we drop this backdrop...and let the sunlight fry 'em!"

The Fire Chief turned and regarded the theatrical backdrop. "Where'd you find this thing?"

Clamp grinned hugely. "It's from a musical I was backing on Broadway. The one about Stalin. It closed last week."

"I thought this thing looked familiar," said the Fire Chief. "I saw that! Boy, that guy could *dance!*"

"Kate?" said Billy Peltzer. He was pacing quickly down a corridor, turning this way and that, looking for his fiancée. "Kate."

Suddenly, a wind storm swept out of the vents, whooshing around him like the Devil himself turned to air.

Chapter
Twenty-two

      Billy Peltzer came awake to the sound of *whirring*.

It was an unpleasant, shrill whirring. The kind of whirring that reminded Billy of—

No. No, it couldn't be. He had been somewhere inside the Clamp building, and now his head hurt real bad, but still and all he could possibly be sitting stretched out in a dentist's chair, about to undergo dental work.

He opened his eyes.

He *was* sitting in a dentist's chair. And that whirring sound—it *was* a dentist's drill.

And holding it was that goofy Gremlin with the name DAFFY stitched to his shirt.

And the dentist drill was coming down toward him!

"Billy!" cried a voice from across the room.

Both Billy and Daffy the Gremlin turned to see a man coming toward them.

It was Murray Futterman!

Mr. Futterman came quickly toward them from the doorway. Daffy turned the drill away from its target in Billy's mouth, and turned it toward the new arrival, aiming for his chest.

But Mr. Futterman dodged. He grabbed hold of the high intensity lamp over the chair, turned it on high, and shone it toward the Gremlin in the dentist's garb.

Daffy shrieked, dropped the drill and ran from the dentist's office.

"You okay, Billy?" asked Mr. Futterman.

"Yeah. Mr. Futterman, what are you doing here?"

"I knew you'd need help, kid. I wasn't gonna let you down. What's next?"

"I was trying to find Kate."

"Right. Let's move it out."

A little woozily, Billy Peltzer followed him, glad to have an ally in this search for Kate.

Somehow, he had the definite feeling that Kate Berringer was in quite a bit of trouble.

Kate Berringer walked down the dim corridor, calling out her fiancé's name. "Billy. Billy!"

She had the feeling that her fiancé was in quite a bit of trouble.

The halls of the Clamp Building, in near darkness, were absolutely creepy pathways to navigate. Thank God she had picked up a flashlight in one of the janitor's offices. She flashed it ahead of her through the musty shadows.

Up ahead, she heard a stirring.

She stepped through a doorway and shone the cone of light about. She picked out a form, caught in some kind of gigantic web stretched from floor to ceiling, wall to wall.

It was Marla Bloodstone, Billy's boss and the woman who had planted that lipstick mark on his cheek!

The struggling woman turned up her head. Her usually perfectly coiffed red hair was a total mess, and her smart business apparel was in absolute shreds. She looked like Tarzan's Jane in one of those old Johnny Weismuller films.

She looked up at the new arrival, and hope spread across her smeared makeup.

"Thank God you're here!"

Kate frowned and gave her a wronged-female look that would crack a mirror at twenty paces. The air got muskier, and things bordered on cat-fight atmosphere.

"I *could* just leave you there. It seems to be good for your attitude."

Marla blinked, and one of her false eyelashes dropped off. "Look—about Billy. Nothing happened. Really. I asked him to go out to dinner with me, but it was just business."

Kate shook her head impatiently. "You don't expect me to believe *that* crock, do you Marla? I know your type, sweetheart." She started to turn and leave.

"No! Don't go!" said Marla desperately, totally stuck onto the web. "Wait. I'm going to be honest with you. It'll be a cathartic openness thing. It wasn't business. I tried to get something going with him. But I couldn't get to first base. Does that help?"

Kate looked at her and for the first time saw something like sincerity on her face. "It'll do."

She reached into the purse slung across her shoulder and pulled out a Swiss army knife. She started working on the web strands with the blade.

Suddenly Marla, looking over her shoulder, saw something.

Something that made her scream.

Kate spun around.

There, standing in the middle of the doorway, blocking the doorway so that there was no hope of escaping was a Gremlin. Only it wasn't just a Gremlin—like an obscene centaur, its upper body was pure evil Gremlin, and the rest of its body was pure hairy, creepy-crawly tarantula-type *spider*.

Kate's scream joined Marla's in an unholy duet as the Spider Gremlin wobbled toward them, leering above its outrageously ugly and hairy body, radiating a predatory nimbleness and dexterity.

Kate realized that the rumbling sound she was hearing was the awful thing's stomach!

"Damn!" she said. She went back to work on the last strand binding Marla, cutting it off. "C'mon!" she ordered. "Run!"

Marla did not have to be encouraged. She'd already kicked off her high-heels and was sprinting right along with Kate.

However, they were going much too fast to notice that the corridor into which they thought they were escaping was strung with more webs. They ran smack into the stuff.

"Oh no!" screeched Marla. "Not again!"

To make matters worse, Kate hit the sticky filaments so hard that she dropped the Swiss army knife. So there went hope of cutting her way out!

And the Spider Gremlin just kept on coming toward them, drool flowing from its mouth, its claws held up before it, ready and eager to pounce.

Yes, it was definite nightmare stuff, the kind of moment usually reserved for nineteen fifties horror movies.

"Billy!" moaned Kate as the spider bore down upon them.

It was the time for action, and Gizmo the Mogwai was just the guy for the job.

With a determined scowl to his features, the Mogwai kicked open the vent and shouldered his way through. He jumped down to a display case, where he had plenty of room to maneuver.

Below him the melodramatic tableau stretched out. Spider Gremlin and women imprisoned in webs.

Yes, time to kick some ass!

He'd had it with these evil creatures. You

could only be so good and so sweet for so
long, and take crap from everybody till you
snap. Then you become a lean, mean action
machine.

Gizmo had known what he had to do.

He'd known, because he'd seen that Sylvester Stallone movie. What was it called? Oh,
yeah. DUMBO! Right.

What Gizmo had done was to find himself
a nice black head band and he'd tied it on
good and tight. Then he'd gotten himself a
bow, just like in the movie, only made out of
good strong paper clips and rubber bands.
And for arrows? Why, safety matches of
course.

Only now he didn't have a helicopter to
blow out of the sky—just a very hairy and
ugly Spider Gremlin.

Yes, he could remember what the muscle
man had said, he knew what to do:

"To survive a war, you've got to *become*
war!"

Determined, Gizmo the Mogwai struck the
match across the wall. It flared alight.

He aimed.....

......and let fly!

They were coming around the bend, an-
swering the screams for help that they'd
heard, when Billy and Murray Futterman saw
the match flaring through the air like a tiny
meteor streaking across a cloudy, dim sky.

They followed this flaming missile and
drew back when they saw the exceedingly

large Gremlin-monster which was its target. What a brute, thought Billy.

Fortunately, however, Gizmo's arrow wasn't just well-aimed. It was very, very effective. It landed on the beast's shoulders and scooted along its back, spreading a trail of fire as it went.

The flames caught.

They caught and they spread.

Within short moments, the stalking Spider Gremlin was a wailing, burning conflagration, twisting legs writhing upwards like twigs in a bonfire. It smelled like burning insects . . .

Scratch one Gremlin, thought Billy.

There were more important matters to deal with, though. He rushed to the aid of the women.

"Oh Billy!" said Kate.

"Oh Billy!" said Marla.

Kate gave Marla a warning look. "There's a Swiss army knife I dropped on the floor."

Billy scooped it up and he cut the women free. Kate beat Marla into his arms.

Murray Futterman was preoccupied with the creature on top of the display case. "What's that?" he wanted to know.

"That's Gizmo, Mister Futterman. He's on our side."

"Okay. Good enough for me." Murray Futterman, showing not a sign of fear, went up and gave Gizmo a hand down. "Uh . . . thanks, Gizmo," he said to the Mogwai.

Gizmo nodded and gave a Sylvester Stallone nod looking tres cool, tres tough.

"Billy," said Kate, pointing at Gizmo and his new get-up. "What happened to him?"

"I guess they—pushed him too far."

"Thank God you're okay," Billy said, looking at Kate with total love and total relief.

"I'm okay now."

Marla was busy digging into the purse she had dropped. She pulled out two cigarettes, lit them both and held them in separate hands, alternating. "Could someone tell me what the *hell* is going on here?"

"Well—" said Billy, "Gizmo got wet and then the Mogwais ate after midnight and then some of the Gremlins must have mutated, because of the genetic material they ate at Splice of Life."

Marla, squinting in the cigarette smoke, could only nod and say, "Oh."

"And if these things get out of here now," Billy continued.

"We'll stop 'em, Billy. I'll tell you something—ever since these guys attacked us, back in Kingston Falls, I've been scared it would happen again." His face was intense, but quite, *quite* victorious. "But now that it's happened . . . I'm not scared."

"How come?" Billy asked, honestly interested. This was a real breakthrough for Mr. Futterman.

Murray Futterman shrugged. "Screwy, huh? But you know, Billy—the most important part of 'American' is those last four letters: 'I can.' Washington didn't give up . . . Lincoln didn't give up—"

"Please!" said Kate. She looked like she was close to tears again.

"What's wrong?" said Murray Futterman.

"I'm sorry, it's—Lincoln's birthday. Something terrible happened on Lincoln's birthday one year and ever since then..."

Oh no. No doubt this story was as bad as her Christmas story about her father... And that one was a lu-lu!

"I don't think we have time, Kate. Let's go!"

He grabbed her and hurried her along before she could do more of the story.

As dear as she was to him, there were much more important things to do now than to listen to Kate Berringer's Lincoln's Birthday story.

Chapter
Twenty-three

They were all ready.

All the Gemlins in the Clamp Center Building, seeing that the hour was drawing close for their foray into the streets of New York (for seven o'clock surely meant that everything was dark outside, right?) had gathered in one large bunch in the lobby.

They were ready all right!

They were ready to *party!*

They were all there, converged in one clamorous, unglamourous troop, like a road show from Hell.

Look! There's George. Oh boy, and there's Lenny, doofing around as usual. Daffy was doing his usual silly cut-ups. A lot of the other Gremlins excitedly clutched tourist paraphernalia and guidebooks, yakking excitedly about what fun they'd have infesting the Empire State building and trashing Grand Central Station.

Finally, the last to enter, Mr. Glasses sauntered on in, absolutely dressed to the nines. He wore a hat, which he took off and tossed into the crowd. He took off his snazzy sportscoat, tossed it over his shoulder, and then twanged his bow tie.

"Is everybody here!" said Mr. Glasses, taking a few dance steps and then gesturing expansively to the crowd.

The Gremlins cheered their assent, eyes glowing with eager anticipation.

"All *right* then!"

He signaled his colleagues and companions to start singing.

"Da da da da da—da da da da da—" began the familiar background support.

And then Mr. Glasses launched into the song made famous by that Italian singer from Hoboken—"New York, New York!"

All the Gremlins swung into the song, dancing about, their varied costumes jangling and swaying as they blissed out like a Busby Berkley chorus line from Mars.

A little farther away, two human types were peeking out from the cover of trash cans with swinging lids. Katsuji followed this new action with his camera, while Grandpa Fred spoke into the microphone like Edward R. Murrow doing World War II from a bunker.

".....it seems incredible, but following their *bloodcurdling rampage of destruction,* these creatures are now mounting what appears to be a production number..."

Up above, on the mezzanine, Billy Peltzer, Kate Berringer, Gizmo and Murray Futterman arrived just in time to view the start of these crazed musical proceedings.

"Hey, these guys aren't bad," said Mr. Futterman.

"Billy—they're going to the doors," said Kate. "They're headed out to New York! They'll be in the streets."

Billy pointed to the dark solarized windows. "It's not really night out there. Mister Clamp just made it look that way. Don't worry. In a few seconds, Mister Clamp's going to drop that cloth out there. The sunlight will come in and—"

There was a rumble of thunder. The darkness outside got darker. There was the sound of a rainburst.

"Sunlight?" said Kate.

Another thunderclap rocked the Clamp Building.

Outside, Daniel Clamp looked up at the clouds shutting down the big power plant in the sky. Too bad he didn't own the sun, he thought, and he sadly waved a "don't bother" signal to the guys holding the backdrop.

Inside, Mr. Glasses cheerfully lead the assembled Gremlins closer to the doors. Pretty soon this would start changing into "Singing in the Rain!"

Some of the Gremlins formed a Rockettes-type kick-line while others hungrily paged through the "Dining after Midnight in New York Guide."

Back up on the mezzanine, Billy and the others watched helplessly. "If those guys get out there in the rain—this town's going under for the third time," said Mr. Futterman.

"Billy, we've got to do something," said Kate.

"I know, I know," said Billy.

And then he had it.

He knew what they had to do.

He pointed to a coiled canvas fire hose in a case on the wall nearby.

"Mr. Futterman. Get that hose. Aim it into the lobby."

"Into the lobby? Are you nuts?"

"Just do it fast. . . . Kate, get a box and put Gizmo in it . . . keep him dry . . ."

Billy turned to Marla, puffing away on yet more cigarettes.

"Marla?"

"Yes?"

"Marla, you *smoke*."

Marla nodded. Yeah, she could do that.

Down in the lobby, Mr. Glasses was still singing up a storm.

On the mezzanine, Kate had found a cardboard box from a nearby shoe store. She put Gizmo in the box.

Mr. Futterman hauled out the hose.

Billy dragged a video-phone extension from a mezzanine office and brought it to Kate, who'd just successfully dealt with the reluctant Gizmo, who only wanted to get into the action.

"Kate," said Billy. "There's a call on hold in Mister Clamp's office. Can you transfer it down here without going up there?"

"Oh God—I think so—"

"Hurry."

"Here, you hold him," said Kate, giving the box to Marla. Marla had to get rid of one of her cigarettes to hold the boxed Mogwai, but she accepted the duty. "Don't let him get wet!" instructed Marla.

"Does it bite?" said Marla.

From the box, Gizmo twittered resentfully.

They were ready to go.

Billy just prayed that his plan would work. Because if it didn't. . . . he didn't want to contemplate what would happen to this city . . .

Let alone the whole country, the whole world.

Down in the lobby a group of the Gremlins spotted them and started climbing a modernistic sculpture to get them.

Time, thought Billy Peltzer, was definitely running out.

"You know where to point the nozzle!" he said to Mr. Futterman.

"Yeah, but I still don't understand."

"You'll see."

"I just hope this works out, Billy. That's all I can say." Mr. Futterman said, pointing the hose toward the dancing, prancing Gremlins in the lobby below.

Billy ran back to the wheel that would turn on the water pressure.

Down below, Mr. Glasses, grinning from ear to ear, totally blissed out at the notion of charging out into the Big Apple, Fun City itself, launched into the breath-taking finale of the big beautifully choreographed Gremlin production number.

"It's up to you, New York, New—"

He reached out to pull open the door that would allow the Gremlin crowd to spill out into the big city, Billy reached the wheel.

At first, it stuck.

Come on, he spat. COME ON!

He put every ounce of strength into the effort.

He spun it.

He could feel the surge of water as it gushed out, filling up the canvas hose into a hard rod. The water pressure hit Murray Futterman like a ton of bricks, but the wiry little guy was determined.

He stood fast, and he directed it down toward the Gremlins climbing the sculpture.

Splooooooooooooooooooooosh!

The spike of water gushed out fast and hard, washing over the Gremlins on the statue like a liquid fist. It knocked them back into the crowd and then the water began to spray out over them like a furious, maniacal water sprinkler.

Following Billy's instructions, Mr. Futterman sprayed the stuff out evenly, making sure *all* of the gremlins got throughly drenched.

And they did.

It was like an artificial, driving rain, and it got George, it got Lenny, it got all the progeny of Mohawk—and first and foremost, it sprayed against Mr. Glasses, knocking the door closed and actually succeeding in shutting the guy up.

Water!

Gremlins turned with great big smiles to catch the spray.

Water!

This was the stuff that, after all, made more Gremlins!

Almost as soon as the things were touched with the stuff, their skins started to bubble.

What a sight!

Murray Futterman kept the water coming, doing just as Billy had instructed, making sure all the Gremlins got a good drenching, but more importantly making sure that there was a connective sheen of water on the lobby floor, a huge puddle connecting all the Gremlins.

Billy went up to the rail. Yes! It was going right! The water was there, give it a few seconds more, just to make sure....

Already, however, he could see the little Gremlins growing out of the bubbles. Smoke and glistening mucus and popping sound, and the smell of suphur and unspeakable Gremlin replication...

No time to waste!

Now to the next part of the program.

He reached over to Kate, who was obeying

her orders, furiously punching into the video-phone's keypad.

"Tap into the PBX . . ." she was reciting like a litany, trying to remember the right way to do it. "Back through the voice mail module . . . main switchboard . . . into the Ethernet . . . five-digit code—"

"That's it!" Billy exclaimed.

It was flashing onto the videophone screen in maddened and furious zapping of electronic frenzy: the Electro-Gremlin. It writhed in agony as the muzak played on and on, Mantovani-hell.

It was trying to get itself off Hold, and Billy Peltzer was going to help it.

Billy grabbed the phone from Kate, lifted the receiver and held it out over the mezzanine railing, over the smoggy, mucusy and disgusting mess of Gremlins giving birth to younglings.

And then pushed the blinking hold button down.

It was then, and only then, that Billy Peltzer witnessed true anarchy, true craziness . . .

True Hell in New York City!

Chapter
Twenty-four

Later, when Billy Peltzer told the story of GREMLINS II: THE NEW BATCH, to his grandchildren, he would of course have to censor things a bit, because the scene that resulted from his unleashing of the Electro-Gremlin was grown-up, X-rated, all-out, full-time ugly.

Joyful to be let loose from its captivity, the Electro-Gremlin naturally rushed out to join in the fun, to be with its buddies again.

And look! His pals were covered in wonderful water, and they were just having one hell of a time, giving birth to lots of little Gremlins.

Of course, the Electro-Gremlin wanted a piece of the action!

It wanted to have babies too!

Babies were *wonderful!*

And so, the Electro-Gremlin dived right into the water.

Of course, as any physicist can tell you (and any victim of a hair-dryer in a full bathtub might tell you as well if they'd survived) water conducts electricity better than Leonard Bernstein conducted the New York Philharmonic.

The Electro-Gremlin dived into that water, all zillions of watts and volts and amps and whatever of him zinging and zapping through the water and meeting the resistance of the molting Gremlins.

The poor Electro-Gremlin shorted out, big time.

But not before the wonderful Gremlin babys were toasted a golden black.

And certainly not before the electricity ran through the adult Gremlins like electron knives slashing through the things at a sub-atomic level ...

... simply disconnecting every cell in their bodies.

The result was, in a word, a true spectacle.

There is a famous story by Edgar Allan Poe entitled "The Curious Case of M. Valdemar." In this gruesome tale, a diseased man is hypnotized, so as to forestall death. When the man dies, he is still able to live and speak, under the will of the hypnotist. However, once the hypnotic spell is broken, the man starts crumbling and melting and oozing pus and more noxious putrescence.

In the movie version he is played by Vincent Price and he just oozes all over Basil Rathbone, who'd been menacing his daughter.

Imagine this, but times several hundred.

They all screamed.

For each of the Gremlins, their bodies riddled with electricity, began to spasm and tremble violently.

And they began to rattle apart, slowly being reduced to their component protoplasm, glopping down messily and greenly into the already wet floor.

Yuccccccckkkkkkkkk!

"Get back!" said Billy, pulling his friend back and pushing the fire hose away.

Kate tripped back and then hugged Billy, holding him closely. "Oh, dear. This reminds of the time . . ."

"Shhh!" said Billy. "Save it for later."

He watched as the Gremlins disintegrated.

The last one to go down was Mr. Glasses, who was slowly dissolving into the Frogs-in-a-blender mess.

When it was all over, when the dead Gremlins had finished the floppings and dissolvings and were just janitor-work, the doors of the Clamp Building burst open and Daniel Clamp himself burst in, leading what he clearly felt would be a last ditch charge of a police SWAT team.

He found nothing but a sea of goo, stretched out over the lobby.

He waved the SWAT team to a stop.

"It's okay, guys." He looked out over the greenish purple sludge which was all that was left of the monsters that menaced his domain. "Maybe we can use this stuff as land fill."

Suddenly, he was confronted by Grandpa Fred in his Dracula costume and Katsuji with his camera. Fred was speaking into his mike. "We're here exclusively with—"

Clamp held his hands up, ordering the duo to stop. "Excuse me there, pa. Who told you to go on my network with all that coverage today?"

"Uhm.... nobody, sir. It just—seemed like news, and I..."

"Right. I'm making you an anchor. Six o'clock weeknights."

Fred Finlay was overwhelmed. "You're making me a news anchor!"

"I want you to go down to Barney's," said Clamp, "and see about some different clothes, though this costume of yours...this says to me, 'Old World.' Think about sweaters. Think avuncular."

"Uh, right," said Fred Finlay.

"Congrats!" said Katsuji. Holding out a hand he shook Fred's hand quickly and then they started backing out of the building together. Katsuji swung the mini-camera back up and focused back onto his favorite reporter.

Katsuji stared straight into the lens, Walter Kronkite redux.

He said, "What does a men's makeover cost

in Manhattan today? Join us as we investigate . . ."

Billy and his friends hurried down the mezzanine. Billy was still a little bit bothered by this gloppy mess here, but he felt pretty darn good anyway.

Clamp saw them coming. He flashed a trademark smile. "Bill, it looks like you bailed us out here . . ."

"It wasn't just me, sir. Everybody helped. Marla here, and—"

Clamp looked at Marla and it was as though it was for the very first time.

"Marla . . . You work for me, don't you!" He smiled and his eyes gleamed with fresh appreciation.

Marla smoothed down her dress modestly, and turned a smoldering, sexy look toward Daniel Clamp. "Yes sir. Very, very hard."

As their gazes locked, sparks seemed to fly.

Billy shook his head, smiling.

Poor Mr. Clamp. Marla's hooks were in him, and dollars to donuts, the only agreement between them, prenuptially speaking, would be the color of the wedding gown.

Another wave of people passed through the doors of the Clamp building. Reporters, mostly. Plus Sheila Futterman, all ga-ga with worry over her poor, dear hubby.

"Murray!" she cried. "What happened?"

Murray Futterman embraced his wife with a manly, happy enthusiasm. "They tried it again, Sheila. But we were ready for 'em." He turned back to Billy and Kate, a big grin on his face. "We're going home, guys. See you...."

"Oh, Murray!" said Sheila Futterman. "You're so brave, so wonderful. I can't wait till we get back home!"

"Neither can I, hon!"

The happy couple waved bye-bye and took off.

"What happened here?" a reporter demanded.

"Oh, it was a complete nightmare disaster," Marla responded. "We had to stop work completely..." She batted her eyes at Daniel Clamp. Clamp smiled back significantly.

"I'm sorry about the building, sir," said Billy Peltzer.

"I'm not!" said Clamp, barely able to keep his eyes off Marla.

Kate said, "You're not?"

"For one thing," said Clamp. "We're insured for the damage. For another...maybe it wasn't for people anyway. It was a place for things. You make a place for things..." He looked around at the cold angles, the stainless steel of the arboretum, the chrome of the bar, the wall to wall linoleum and tile with its great big green boo-boo still gloppily spreading. "You make a place for things...things come."

"Well, you kept the city safe," said Billy.

"That's right. That's a good point. The sacrifice.... you know, this could be good in my next book. I should be taking notes. You have any paper?"

"Let me see."

He rummaged in his trouser pocket and came up with a paper and a pencil.

Clamp unfolded the paper. "Wait a minute. What's this?"

Billy suddenly remembered what that paper was. It was the drawing he was working on . . . The drawing of the main street of Kingston Falls.

"That's Kingston Falls," said Kate.

Clamp struck the corner of the thing with the back of his hand, a great big grin coming to his face. "This is what I'm looking for."

Billy blinked. "You want to move there?"

"I want to *build* it. My new project, over in Jersey—this is terrific! This is what people want now—the traditional community thing. Quiet little towns! Back to the earth—" He indicated the drawing. "Is this your concept?"

"It's our home town!" said Kate.

"That's even better. I love that! It's—wait— *Clamp Corners!*" Clamp traced an imaginary banner across the sky. 'Where life slows down to a crawl.' What do you think?"

"Uh, that's—"

"It's terrific," said Kate.

"This is the kind of thing people need. Not talking elevators, just—Bill, you sell me this design, and we'll build the biggest, most sensationally quiet little town you've ever *seen.*"

"What you want, of course, is for Billy to design the whole *town,*" snapped Kate.

"We can come to a deal. Believe me. Are you Mrs. Peltzer?" Clamp inquired.

Kate smiled and leaned against Billy's arm. "I'm going to be. Yeah."

He squeezed Kate tighter and little Gizmo, giving up the Rambo mode, became cuddly little Gizmo the Mogwai again, glowing with softness and furry love.

Clamp looked down at Gizmo. He seemed moved.

"It's funny—I look at him, and you know what I see?"

Kate said, "What?"

"I see dolls with suction cups looking out of cars. I see a big balloon in the Macy's parade. Has anyone talked to you about merchandising?"

Billy shook his head, bewildered. "To me? No."

"There's definitely something here. Maybe lose the headband."

Suddenly Gizmo was back in his macho mode again. He twittered a definite, 'No way, bud!'

"He likes the headband," explained Billy.

"It's flexible, Bill."

Gizmo felt free to relax and cuddle some more.

"Excuse me," said Clamp. He stepped over, straightening his tie. There were more reporters to talk to.

He left Billy and Kate and Gizmo to do just that.

Gizmo gibbered a cluster of indecipherable Mogwai words at Billy.

Billy got the message.

"Okay," he said to the little guy.

"You understand him?" asked Kate.

Billy blinked and then smiled. Yes, he *did* understand the little fellow. Maybe that's what Mister Wing had been talking about . . .

Maybe this meant he was growing up.

"Well," said Kate impatiently. "What did he say?"

"He said he wants to go home."

"Where's home?"

Gizmo twittered again, and this time there could be no question about what he was saying.

Billy smiled warmly at the love of his life, his very own sweet fiancée, Kate Berringer.

"Our place!"

Kate's eyes, warm already, simply melted.

Billy pulled her close to him and, together, they went outside, carrying Gizmo in his box along with them.

Marla was loving this.

First, Mister Clamp heavily noticing her—
—and now, she was getting to actually talk to reporters.

She posed for them in her chic shredded office suit, showing her pearly whites for their flashing cameras.

". . . and then," she explained, "some of the Mogwais apparently ate after midnight, and whenever *that* happens . . ."

Meanwhile, Clamp himself was still dealing with the reporters in his usual cool, controlled manner.

"Yes, and then, my superb employee, Bill Peltzer had a brilliant conceptual extrapolation and he—"

Clamp was interrupted by an assistant, carrying a cellular phone over to him.

"It's for you, sir. From here in the building."

"In the building?" Daniel Clamp took the phone. Who could still be in the building? Who could have survived? Whoever it was must have gone through absolute hell!

He took the phone.

"Hello?"

Pause. And then the voice came to him and his eyebrows shot up with surprise.

"Forster! What are you—okay, okay, we'll get you out of there. Which floor? Wow, way up there. No, it'll take a while, the elevators are out and the lobby is . . . I don't know, not too long. . . . we'll do what we can Forster. Just keep your pants on!"

He smiled at the reporters. "Looks as though we have another employee in a bit of a jam."

Frank Forster had met his Waterloo.

He'd managed to escape to a conference room all the way near the top of the building, but she'd followed him.

The Gremlin in the Dress . . .

"What a hunk!" she was saying as she closed in on him. "Don't be afraid of what you feel!"

Forster was back in the room as far as he could go.

And she was coming for him.

"No," he whimpered. "Please!"

"I need you, Frank. Is that wrong?"

She was undulating toward him, her hips pumping beneath her tight sequined dress, her breasts thrust out before her like offerings. Her lips worked in kissy-kissy motion, hungry for him.

"Roll over me with your hot love. . . . What about my needs? Intimacy. . . . We never talk. Why can't you commit?"

Daniel Clamp hung up, leaving him all alone.

She was coming for him . . .

Frank Forster looked down at the Gremlin with the Dress and the breasts and her long purple hair.

He shrugged and closed his eyes and sank into surrender onto the floor.

"Please be gentle," he said.